MW00960458

Where We Met

Nicole Baker

Copyright © 2023 by Nicole Baker

All rights reserved.

No portion of this book may be reproduced in any form without written permission from the publisher or author, except as permitted by U.S. copyright law.

Edited by: Kati Kellnhauser Editing and Brooke's Editing Services

Contents

Chapter One

Savannah

A loud boom sounds above me, coming through the ceiling of my new apartment.

"Shit!" I whisper to myself as I look around for my keys.

There's yelling going on in the apartment upstairs, something I've already become accustomed to in the week that I've lived here.

My dog Bailey looks up at me with a concerned face. I kneel down and scratch her favorite spot right behind her ears.

"It's okay, girl," I tell her soothingly. "I've gotta go to class, but I'll be back soon." I kiss her on the head and walk out, locking up behind me.

I hate having to leave her here alone. Except for work, I haven't gone anywhere all week, but today is my first day back at school. My first two classes were earlier in the day, officially kicking off the last semester of my senior year, and now I've just got one last lecture today.

I decided to come home for a couple of hours in between, having no desire to spend more time on campus. As soon as I got to my apartment, I regretted that decision. It just isn't home.

It's a world of difference from where I lived on campus with my friends last semester.

My dad got remarried a few months ago to Veronica, my step-mom, and has been struggling to keep up with extra costs. Veronica has two kids from a previous marriage. They're much younger than me, being in first and third grade. Dad's been distracted and overwhelmed by having to support three extra people, especially two kids who live under his roof now. But he's happy, so I'm happy for him.

When he asked if I could swing paying a portion of my rent on my own, I felt so bad that I told him I could cover all of it.

Turns out, that wasn't true at all. But instead of owning up to my mistake, I decided to move out. The only place I could find within my budget is less than ideal, has neighbors who scream at each other incessantly, and is definitely in a dangerous part of town.

It's not advisable to walk alone in this neighborhood, but the closest parking spot I could find after my shift last night was two streets away, and wanting to get back to Bailey after a long day, I took it.

Keep your head down.

That's what I keep telling myself when I walk the streets of this neighborhood. I don't know if it's the right move, but it makes me feel safer.

As soon as I get into my car, I lock the doors and start the engine.

On my drive to class, I pass by the campus coffee shop, longing for my favorite vanilla latte. It's something I wish I could allow myself to indulge in, but I know I can't afford it.

My dad would kill me if he knew I was living like this, but I want him to be happy. We lost my mother to cancer when I was three, and it's just been me and him ever since. He's spent my whole life making sure I had everything I needed. If slumming it for a semester is how I can repay him, it's the least I can do.

Pulling up to the building, I let out a sigh of relief when I notice there's a parking spot open in the front row. Thankfully, I won't have to walk far in this freezing Cleveland weather.

I'm majoring in Marketing with a focus in International Business. I knew I wanted, *needed* to have international travel built into my career. I love meeting people from different backgrounds, and exploring different cultures and seeing how we all operate differently is what makes me feel alive.

I'm a few minutes early to my Managing Cultural Differences class, and when I walk into the lecture hall, my stomach drops when I see familiar faces seated in the front.

"Savannah, hey, over here." Aubrey waves. "Guys, look who's in our class!"

The rest of my friends, the same girls I lived with last semester, turn their heads. They wave and smile as I start to make my way down the stairs.

I haven't called them since I've been back from winter break and moved into my new place. I knew they would ask about it, and I don't want anyone to see where I'm living. They would freak out and demand they help me out.

I'm committed to being the happy, optimistic friend. Growing up without a mother, I've always been the one everyone was worried about and I'm sick of it. I don't want anyone to turn me into a charity case.

"Get over here." Shannon grabs me and brings me into a huge hug. "I've been meaning to call. I wanna come over and see your new place."

There it is. The reason I've been avoiding everybody. We were living in a nice house on campus, and there was just no way I was going to be able to swing that kind of monthly rent with my catering job. So, I told them I had to move out because my dad had to cut back on how much he was able to help me out. I just never told them how bad it actually was.

"Oh, it's nothing worth seeing. I don't even really have much furniture yet." I wave my hand, trying to act nonchalant, hoping she won't press the matter.

I'm actually sleeping on a blow-up mattress, and I put together a piece of crap futon to use as a couch in the living area.

Shannon smiles. "No biggie. Just let us know when it's ready, and we'll plan a girls' night."

"I didn't know you guys were taking this class," I tell them as I take a seat.

"We wanted to get one more class all together before we graduate. This was the only one left in the business college that we could all get credit for toward our own degrees," Aubrey explains.

"How was your winter break?" Tricia asks me.

It was my first Christmas with my new family.

It *has* been a bit of an adjustment, if I'm being honest. For the longest time, it was just me and my dad. I don't remember my mom, but the many photos I have of her prove she was a beautiful, full-of-life woman. My dad has always said that I get my sense of adventure and desire to explore the world from her, and it makes me happy to know that I'm so much like her.

"It was good. Nice to be home," I say. "How about you?"

She shrugs her shoulders. "Can't complain. My parents got along for once, and my sisters were tolerable."

I bend down to get my laptop out of my bag and set it on my desk.

"Hello, everybody. Welcome to Managing Cultural Differences. My name is Lucas Giannelli, but you all can call me Professor Luke."

I hear a low gasp come from Aubrey while Shannon and Tricia giggle next to me. I'm about to ask them what's so funny when I look up at the front of the room.

I'm hit with quite possibly the sexiest man I've ever laid eyes on. His dark hair is cut short on the sides and left a little longer on the top. He has green eyes that pop against his olive skin, and his short beard makes him look like someone who belongs on the cover of a magazine.

Who is this guy?

I would have known if there was a professor this sexy walking around campus, especially if he's part of the International Business program.

My heart starts to accelerate, and I find myself sitting up straighter as I fix my hair.

What am I doing? He's my *professor*.

"Now, I know some of you are taking this class as an elective for business, but some of you are International Business majors. By a show of hands, who here is majoring in International Business?" he asks.

I raise my arm and look around to see only about twenty others raising their hand. Most of my peers took the class last year, but like I said, I wanted an easy senior year.

Professor Luke scans the room as he evaluates how many of us are majoring in International Business. I'm usually not one to squirm at the attention of a man, good-looking or not, but I feel my body tingle the second his eyes land on mine.

He looks almost surprised at the sight of me, letting his gaze linger on me for a moment. I sit up straight and don't allow my stare to waver. When he finally tears his glance away, I'm not sure if I'm imagining it, I manage to convince myself that I'm probably just making it up in my head.

I need to get a hold of myself. This isn't like me.

"To my right, you will find your TA for the semester, Rebecca. She will be assisting with grading papers and answering any questions you may have along the way. While Rebecca passes out the syllabus, I will tell you a little bit about myself. Like I said, my name is Lucas Giannelli, and I own Giannelli Family Selections with my siblings. We travel the world tasting the finest wines you can imagine, looking for the best of the best to recommend to our clients around the country."

Not only is he gorgeous, but he's cultured too? My libido is taking a hit right now. Is it hot in here? I look around at everyone else, all perfectly content in their seats. Meanwhile, my body feels like it's burning up.

Professor Luke starts walking closer to my side of the room as he continues.

"I still work full-time with my siblings but am here at your university to help fill this role until they find another professor. I'm honored to be able to share what I've learned in my travels with you guys. Now some of you are here to fill in some credits, and that's okay, but for the others..." he says just as his eyes fall to me, and I swear there is some kind of electricity buzzing between us. "I'm here to answer any and all questions. I want you to learn as much as you can from what I've experienced in my career over the years."

As the syllabus stack for my aisle reaches me, I grab one and pass it down the line.

Professor Luke starts to read it over and I do my best to pay attention to his words and not the man speaking them.

"In this class, we will go over many different techniques for how to work with people from different backgrounds. All of what we learn will be geared toward your final assignment, where you will be partnered up with an overseas university student, given a real-world issue faced by companies, and work together to find a solution."

I'm bursting with excitement at the thought of being connected with someone overseas. I can't help but wonder who I am going to get and what country they'll be from.

I've never left the country before, but I've always wanted to, hence my future career choice.

Professor Luke looks my way as I smile, excitement filling me. I think I see the start of a smile form on his face, but it's gone in a second.

Again, I must be imagining things.

I observe him while he continues his lecture. His dark jeans fit his body exquisitely, his crisp white shirt underneath a brown jacket doing absolutely nothing to hide the lean muscles of his upper body.

"Finally, before we get started with today's lesson, I want to announce something. Your spring break is just about two months from now. This just so happens to coincide with a very important meeting I have with a potential client in Italy."

I look over at Rebecca, who smiles at the class. She seems sweet enough, very pretty. Her long red hair is full, falling in gorgeous waves down to her breasts. I wonder if she gets to spend a lot of one-on-one time with Professor Luke, and I am hit with an unwarranted pang of jealousy.

"Two weeks before break, you will be given a written exam that will be graded by Rebecca. The highest score on the exam will be accompanying me to my meeting in Italy for some real, hands-on experience in international business."

Based on the high-fives, whistling, and cheering going on around me, it's clear everybody here wants a free trip to Italy. I have no doubt every girl in the class is dying to get a chance to spend a week with our professor.

A whole week in Italy! The idea of it alone has me wanting to do cartwheels down the hall. I get out my to-do list and add *get a passport*. Just in case, by some miracle, I happen to win.

While Professor Luke proceeds to our class material, I can't help but fantasize about what a trip to Italy with him might be like. Trying new wines, eating pasta, and indulging in gelato. Meeting the owners of wineries and learning all about how they make their wine... It sounds like a dream.

My mission for the semester is clear: win this trip of a lifetime.

Chapter Two

Luke

"Looks like we're out of time today. I look forward to spending this semester with you. See you all on Wednesday," I say as the students begin to pack up their things.

I made it. My first time teaching a class, and I survived.

When my buddy Eric, a full-time professor here in the business department, asked me to fill the role of adjunct professor for a class in this semester's International Business program, I was shocked.

It's honestly a lot of extra work on top of my already incredibly demanding role at the company, but I was honored to be asked. I enjoy what I do, love it actually, and I hope I can pass on some useful information to my students.

It's going to be a hectic five months doing both jobs until this class ends in May, but I'm up for the challenge.

I swore to my siblings this wouldn't interfere with my normal duties for the company, and I'm determined to keep my promise. So, if that means waking up at four a.m. on Monday, Wednesday, and Friday to make it into the office and get my tasks done before leaving early to teach this class, so be it.

As I pack up my brown leather briefcase, made from real Italian leather that I got in Milan, my eyes move on their own accord to the blonde beauty sitting in the front row.

She's packing up her things while her friends are laughing and chatting around her. There's something different about her, making her seem different than the rest of the girls in class. When I mentioned the idea of a trip to Italy, she didn't react like the other students. I saw her real enthusiasm at the idea of getting paired with an international student for her project.

I appreciate the fact that her eyes lit up from hearing she'll be connecting with someone from another country. It's a passion of mine too, and the real reason I wanted to teach this class was to encourage people to do the same.

"You did such a great job." Rebecca approaches my desk. "That's so kind of you to bring a student with you to Italy. I think most girls are going to be studying their little hearts out for a chance to spend a week alone with you," she says, her eyes fluttering at me.

I shrug my shoulders. "I'm sure all of my students will study hard for the assignment. It's a big opportunity for all of them, not just the girls."

She laughs. "Oh, Lucas. You have a lot to learn about women if you believe that. I'll see you in class on Wednesday. I'm looking forward to working closely with you."

I don't like her insinuating that only my female students are excited for a chance to go to Italy simply because it'll be with me. I've been told enough times that I'm a good-looking guy to know that it's true, but I think these students are more interested in experiencing the trip of a lifetime rather than being near me.

As I walk to my car, I pull my phone out and call my brother Marcus. He's one of my three siblings, and the youngest of the three boys. I'm the middle son, Gabriel is the oldest, and Mia is our baby sister.

"Hello, Professor Lucas," Marcus says with humor in his tone. "Mia and I are just sitting here in my office brainstorming how we can sneak into your class and see how in the world anyone with half a brain would ever take you seriously."

I shake my head when I hear Mia chuckle in the background. "You're fucking hilarious," I say sarcastically.

"Leave him alone," Mia defends. "How did it go?"

As I take a seat in my Mercedes, the smooth sound of the engine comes to life. I don't usually care to spend my money frivolously, but getting this car was something I did for myself. I've worked my ass off, along with my siblings, to make our company what it is today.

"It went well, thank you very much. There's a good amount of International Business majors that I think will get a lot out of my class."

For some reason, the mention of the students has me picturing *her* again. I see beautiful women all the time, so I really don't know what has gotten into me, why I couldn't take my eyes off her during class. Why I can't stop thinking about her now.

I try to shake the thoughts from my mind, reminding myself that I need to be professional. I'm her teacher, for God's sake.

"I'm sure they will. You're a good man, especially for doing this simply as a favor, free of charge to the university," Mia adds.

"And you get to be around young, hot college chicks," Marcus says.

"Ugh, you're so gross," Mia scolds him.

"What? How am I gross? It's not like we're fifty."

That's Marcus for you. Being the youngest son in the family, he's always had the freedom to be who he wants, to say whatever comes to mind—something he takes full advantage of.

As for me being the middle child, my parents were busy basking in the glory of Gabe's success while oohing-and-aahing over the cuteness of Marcus and Mia. I was stuck in between, somewhere lost in the shuffle, just trying to make everybody happy. My sole goal had always been to not rock the boat.

"We may not be fifty, but we're definitely not twenty-one anymore," I reply.

Marcus is only twenty-eight compared to my thirty-five, but he's still old enough to make it weird to be drooling over college students.

"Okay, moving on!" Mia interrupts.

"What was the point of this phone call?" I sigh.

"I can't remember. I think we were supposed to see how your first day went," Marcus says. "Ma suggested something about being a supportive brother when she called me this morning."

"Ma should know you're not capable of such mature actions," I tease. "I'm almost home and need to take Vino for a walk. Thanks for all the *support*."

I hang up with my siblings and shake my head as I drive, knowing only the four of us fully understand our dynamic. We do a lot of teasing, but there's nothing but love there.

When I get home, I'm immediately greeted by my golden retriever. Her tail is going crazy as she circles me, knowing our routine well enough to know her leash is about to come out.

"Hey, Vino." I squat down to give her some scratches. "You ready for a walk?"

I pull my winter jacket tighter around my neck as I open the front door and lead her outside. January in Cleveland is brutal, but I try to keep Vino active despite the bitter cold.

I live in a nice suburb called Shaker Heights, which is conveniently close to the city and our family office. I originally chose the location because it's only about a ten-minute drive to Little Italy, which is where I grew up, and my parents still live.

My neighborhood is over one hundred years old, evident by the large trees that line the streets, branches offering a nice shade in the summer, and beautiful leaves in the fall.

I only last about five minutes on the walk before I decide Vino's moved around enough, and I start jogging back home. As soon as I scoop her food into her bowl, I grab the bottle of 2016 Fontodi Chianti Classico from one of the many vendors we buy from in Italy. Giving myself a generous pour, I make my way into the kitchen to find something for dinner.

I'm not a huge fan of eating out, seeing no appeal in wasting money on food that isn't half as good as I can prepare or anywhere near healthy. The more I've forced myself to cook my own food, the easier it's gotten over the years.

Now I can whip up a shrimp linguine with fresh lemon and olive oil in fifteen minutes.

Vino and I sit in front of the stone fireplace as I finish my glass of wine. As I read through the course material handed down to me by the business department, I try to figure out exactly how I'm going to keep the class engaged on Wednesday. I don't want to spew a bunch of bullshit while half of the students drift off into fantasyland.

I've been more than fortunate with my own success over the last two years, and I want to give back. Teaching one lecture may not seem like a lot, but it feels more rewarding than writing a check, which is all I've been able to do up until this point.

I don't know what it is about this experience, but something tells me I'm exactly where I'm meant to be.

Chapter Three

Savannah

"That brings us to the final section of this case study. Can someone tell me why the American businessman is going to fail in bringing this French person on as a client?" Professor Luke asks the class.

It's been two weeks since the semester started, and I still can't seem to shake my body's reaction to Professor Luke. I'm not sure if it's just me, but I feel like his eyes linger on me throughout the entire ninety minutes of each class.

"Yes, go ahead," he calls on a girl on the other side of the room.

"Well, for starters, the entire sales pitch was awful. The French are classy and sexy," she says in a seductive voice, clearly not subtle in her attempt to flirt with our professor. "They would be bored to death with that kind of pitch. I would know, I'm a Marketing major."

Ugh, I do everything in my power not to roll my eyes at her. It's moments like this where I hate myself for this stupid crush I have on him, because obviously every girl in this lecture hall is feeling it too. It's pathetic.

"Um, okay…" Professor Luke responds slowly. "While you may disagree with the sales pitch, we are looking for reasons why this would not sit well with the French businessman because of the cultural differences that the American did not take into account. Anyone else care to answer?"

When the class remains silent, I raise my hand out of annoyance. It's not like we're dealing with rocket science here.

His eyes land on mine. "Yes, go ahead."

"I think there are several reasons why the French businessman or *woman*" —I swear the corner of his mouth turns up at my point— "wouldn't be interested in this deal. For starters, it sounds like the deal is a high-risk situation, and as you stated earlier, the French are not known for being risk-takers in the business world. The American presented his pitch with a cold demeanor, and he didn't add any flair with his personality. He also made it apparent that overtime was a huge factor in the success of the proposal, while the French put work/life balance as a higher priority than working extra hours."

Tricia nudges my side and whispers, "Damn, girl. You sound hot when you talk all intellectual like that."

"That's right," he replies. "What's your name?"

"Savannah."

His eyes warm as he gives me a nod, leaving my stomach in flutters. I'm proud of my response, being as I pulled from very subtle things we've learned so far about French culture in this class, yet he skips over my answer like it was nothing.

I struggle to remain focused as he continues his lecture, hung up on why he didn't have a response or elaborate on my answer.

Luckily, I'm interested enough in this material to rebound quickly. I diligently take notes, excited for our first test next week. Professor Luke goes on to explain how the tests will all be in the form of essay questions and that they'll be graded by Rebecca and approved by him.

"And that's about all the time we have for today. I'll see you all next week," he says as he wraps up class.

I stand up and stretch my arms above my head. Sitting in this chair for ninety minutes always makes my muscles tense. When I steal a glance at Professor Luke, his eyes are on me. As soon as he notices I'm looking at him, he looks down at his shoes.

Just then, an arm wraps around my waist, dragging my attention away from whatever just happened. "Are you up for happy hour with us at Mac's?" Tricia asks.

The local campus bar is known for being strict with IDs, so you're sure not to have to deal with younger classmen trying to sneak in and turn it into some obnoxious place to get wasted.

"I'm down. I need a cold beer to cool me off after watching Mr. Hottie down there strut his stuff." Aubrey fans herself.

I laugh. "Do you think Matt would like you talking about our professor that way?"

Aubrey shrugs her shoulders like it's not a big deal. "Oh, please. Matt knows I love him. That doesn't mean I can't enjoy the view when I'm presented with another beautiful creature."

Shannon's head falls back in laughter. "He's not a character from an alternate world like in your fantasy books."

"Oooh, I wasn't even thinking about that. I'm totally going to picture him like that next class," Aubrey jokes.

As soon as we get to the door of the building, I put on my cream-colored beanie and get my matching gloves out. Even though the bar is on campus, I'm not walking there in this cold.

"Any of you guys need a ride to Mac's?" I offer.

All three of them raise their hands.

"Lucas," someone calls from behind us.

We all turn our heads as one of the other professors in the business department runs up to Professor Luke, who is walking our way.

Professor Eric is also easy on the eyes. I've never had him for class before, but I've seen him around campus.

"I think I have a new kink," Tricia whispers.

She doesn't need to explain what's going on in her head. I'm pretty sure we're all thinking the same thing: that seeing these two attractive professors walk side by side is straight out of a porno.

Professor Luke looks at us as they pass by, nodding his head in our direction. "Ladies."

"Okay, let's get to the bar. We all need a drink," I say.

It only takes us ten minutes to pile into my car and drive to the bar. When we walk in, I look around the room for an empty spot to snag. I see a high-top table in the back and make a beeline for it before anybody else can get there.

The bar is already starting to fill up as students are finishing their Friday classes. I happen to have this Friday off work, which usually doesn't happen with my catering job, so this night comes as a much-needed break.

"Okay, I'm going to go get us all whatever's on tap." Shannon drops her things on a chair and walks toward the bar.

"I'll come help," Tricia says as she follows.

I look around at the crowd, enjoying the feeling of being out and about again. I've been kind of distant the last two weeks as I've been trying to figure out my new normal in my new apartment and newfound life of being dirt-poor.

"Holy shit." Aubrey nudges my arm. "Look who just walked in."

I glance across the room and my heart rate immediately picks up as I see our two professors walk into the bar. I watch on as Professor Luke motions his head to the bar and Professor Eric makes his way toward us in the back, all the way to the high-top table next to ours. He grabs a seat and takes out his phone while he waits.

Aubrey's eyes are opened wide as her lips form a small smirk. She mouths *oh my God* in my direction and I do my best to ignore her.

"Did you guys see who's at the bar?" Tricia laughs as her and Shannon place our beers down.

Before any of us can say anything, Professor Luke walks up to the table next to us with two beers in his hand. I motion my eyes for Tricia to look next to us so she doesn't say something stupid and make us look like idiots.

Shannon holds up her beer for a cheers, managing to ignore the two hotties next to us. She never lets a good-looking man phase her. She's much too spirited and energetic to let such a thing change her mood. I'm usually not too far behind her with her nonchalant way of living, but with Professor Luke in the vicinity, all bets are off.

"To our final semester together..." Shannon starts. "May we enjoy our time together and always cherish the friendships we've made along the way. Cheers!"

"Cheers!" We all join in and clink our glasses together.

The beer goes down smoothly as the cold contents hit the back of my throat. I can't help but glance next to me, watching as Professor Luke laughs at something his friend says. In that moment, I make it my goal for tonight to rid myself of these stupidly inappropriate feelings this man brings out of me.

Shannon notices me eyeing the table next to us and I instantly know she's going to do something stupid when she winks at me.

She turns around in her chair. "Hey, Professor Luke."

Shit. She really has no shame.

"Hi," he responds to her, looking around the table. "You four are in my class, aren't you?"

"You got that right. I'm Shannon." She smiles and extends her arm for a handshake. "I look forward to winning the trip to Italy. I could use some Italian men in my life."

The two men laugh at her brazen remark.

"You're awfully confident. How do your friends feel about you claiming victory so early?" Professor Luke smiles at me.

I grin and look down at my lap.

Shannon shrugs. "We're all adults here. I think they can handle a little friendly competition."

"I told you that trip was going to make these kids go crazy." Professor Eric gives Luke a stare that says *I told you so*.

"Whatever I can do to make the semester more exciting," Luke says.

"So, what year are you ladies?" Eric asks.

"We're seniors. This is our last semester," Aubrey chimes in.

"Good for you. What are your majors?" Eric asks, seeming genuinely interested.

Everyone tells him their major until it gets to me. "Oh, um, I'm International Business."

Eric glances between me and Luke. "You'll learn a lot from this one over here. He's brilliant at what he does and has a wealth of knowledge to offer," Eric tells me. "Anyone majoring in International Business would be crazy not to take advantage of having this man as their professor."

I know what he's saying, I really do, but I mean *come on*. All I can think about is taking advantage of him in ways that have nothing to do with education.

Professor Luke shakes his head while a smile remains on his face. "He's talking me up, but I'm excited to be teaching your class this semester. I'd be happy to answer any questions you may have for me, even if they don't come up organically in class. All my information is in the syllabus."

"That's really kind of you," I reply. "Thanks."

"The offer is on the table to all of you," Professor Eric adds. "I'm here to answer any questions too."

After a couple more minutes of friendly conversation, we let them get back to their conversation.

"Anyone else want to take Professor Hottie up on his offer to contact him for any *questions*?" Shannon whispers mischievously.

I squirm in my seat at the thought of her and Professor Luke spending time together.

"Come on, guys." I lean into the table in an effort to make sure my words are only heard by them. "He's right there."

Their shoulders shake in a fit of laughter.

"What has gotten into you? You're being so buttoned up and… shy. I've never seen you like this," Tricia says. "I think you *like like* Professor Hottie."

I laugh awkwardly, pretending that their words are so ridiculous that I can't contain myself at the hilarity of it all and hoping like hell they aren't seeing right through me.

"You guys are insane. He's our professor," I mouth. "Anyway, tell me about this new guy you said keeps texting you, Trish."

That's called deflecting. It's probably so embarrassingly obvious what I'm doing that my friends just decide to throw me a bone and pretend they fell for it.

Either way, the attention is off me and my inappropriate crush. I almost think I can focus on the girls and not on the professor sitting mere feet away from me.

I can't stop myself from stealing glances at him through the night, though, and every time I look over, I catch his eyes on me. If they aren't on me when I look, they eventually work their way back in my direction.

Okay, get your shit together, Savannah. No more looking at your professor.

"I need to go to the bathroom," I tell my friends. I stand up, and as I move toward the back of the bar, I feel a hand grab my elbow.

"What's up, beautiful?" the male voice breathes into my ear. His breath wreaks of cheap liquor. I look up and see my ex's face. Ugh, he's the last person I want to deal with right now.

"Hi, Miles."

We dated for like four months last year. When I saw him getting a little handsy with a sorority girl at a party, I decided I needed to end our casual relationship. There were no hard feelings for either of us.

"You're looking good," he slurs, still holding onto my arm.

I try to pull it away, but he just tightens his grip.

"Can I have my arm back?" I ask, irritated.

He ignores my question, which makes me start to wonder what the hell I ever saw in him. I feel him pull me toward his body. "I miss you, Sav."

I try again to pull my arm free but have no success.

"Miles, let go of me," I raise my voice at him.

"Hey, buddy," a deep voice echoes from behind me. "The lady said to let her go. I suggest you listen."

Luke steps forward until he's right beside me, and Miles looks suspiciously between me and Luke.

"Is this your new guy?" Miles spits out. "He looks a little old for you."

He lets go of my arm and I immediately start massaging the sore spot where his thumb was digging into me. Luke notices and I see his eyes grow dark.

"That's none of your business, Miles. Please just walk away. You're in no condition to talk right now."

He seems to ponder my words before he finally takes a step back. "I'll see you around campus," he says while holding Luke's eyes, then walks away.

Luke looks me up and down with concern. "Are you okay?"

Miles never acted like that while we were together, so I'm a little shook up by his aggressive demeanor.

"I'm fine," I say with more certainty than I'm feeling at the moment. "I'm sorry you had to see that. I'm so embarrassed."

"Don't be. He's the one who should be embarrassed."

I'm not sure what to say to that, and after standing in awkward silence for a moment, I panic. "I'm gonna head to the bathroom. Thanks for your help," I blurt out, regretting it immediately.

"No problem at all. I'll see you in class, Savannah." He gives me a warm smile then walks to the bar.

I speed walk to the bathroom and push through the door, embarrassed my professor had to witness something like that. If he was able to guess that Miles was an ex-boyfriend, he must think I'm an idiot for dating someone like him. I bet he only dates sophisticated woman who would never find themselves in a situation like that.

God, I just want to erase that from my memory.

I use the restroom quickly, then wash my hands and splash water on my face, hoping the cold water will help me shake it off.

When I get back to our table, I see Luke and Eric are shaking hands and leaving the bar already, having only come for a quick beer. The feeling of regret hits me at having lost my chance to talk to him again.

Chapter Four

Luke

"Hey, Ma," I answer my phone as I walk along the path in the park with Vino on her leash.

"Lucas Giannelli. Why have you been avoiding my calls?" Ma scolds.

My head falls back with frustration. Ma is your stereotypical intrusive Italian mother. She's Marie Barone from Everybody Loves Raymond. She loves with all her heart but doesn't have a clue when she's crossing a line.

"Ma, I haven't been avoiding you. I've been busy. When I get home at night, I'm either exhausted, or I have a lesson to put together for class."

She curses in Italian under her breath. "I told you this would be too much for you. Why don't you ask Marcus to take on some of your responsibilities at the company?"

"I never said it was too much. I said I was busy. There's a difference. Plus, I promised Marcus and Gabe that this class wouldn't interfere with my normal work schedule."

I knew it was going to be a crazy couple of months, and I may be a little extra tired in the evenings, but I'm okay with that. I just have to find enough energy to call Ma at night so I can keep her off my back.

"Just promise me you won't overdo it. You already put in too much time at work as it is," she says.

"I promise."

"Good. So, tell me, how are classes going?"

A squirrel scurries past us, making Vino try to veer off the path to follow it. I have to jerk her back so we don't end up in the grass. She is getting pretty antsy with this winter weather dragging on, as are most people here. Today isn't so bad with the temperature at least above freezing, which is why we are taking this long walk in the park.

"Classes have been great. I feel like I've got a good handle on the material and have been able to add in some lessons of my own that I think add value to the course. I'm glad I took the gig. It feels good to give back somehow. I know the success I've hit at my age has been the luck of the draw. This helps ease some of that guilt."

Imposter syndrome. That's what I feel like I've been contending with, especially for the first couple of years of success. It wasn't until this past year that I've come to terms with the fact that I may actually be good at what I do, better than most.

"Oh, my Lucas. You've always doubted yourself. When are you going to realize how amazing you are?"

"I'm fine, Ma. You worry too much. Listen, I'm at the park with Vino. Can I call you back when I get home?" I ask.

There's really no reason to get off the phone. I just know once she gets on this topic, it goes on forever.

"You better call. I will show up at your house next time. Good-bye, sweetheart."

I sigh. "Bye, Ma. Love you."

I put my phone in my pocket as my brain starts working overtime.

I don't know why she always thinks I'm too hard on myself. It's just in my nature to worry about others first, but that isn't a bad quality to have.

I'm lost in my thoughts, not paying attention to Vino or anything around me, when I feel the leash jerk me forward. Before I know what's happening, I'm being pulled to the other side of the path and am tangled up with another dog and a woman.

Vino and the other dog are jumping around each other in excitement as their leashes continue to twist together.

"Vino," I yell. "Calm down. I'm so sorry, I wasn't paying attention when—" I stop talking when I look up.

It's her. The girl in my class. Savannah.

The one who occupied my mind all last night with her captivating smile and alluring eyes.

"It's okay." She smiles at me. "Bailey, sit."

Both dogs listen to her command as we lean down to untangle them. I'm mere inches from her mouth, her hair is down and blowing into my face. It smells like vanilla and something else... maybe some kind of flower. Whatever it is, it makes my dick twitch.

I make quick work to let go of Vino's leash and unravel it from the other one so I can stand back up and get some distance.

"We keep running into each other," she says with a hint of shyness to her voice. It's sweet and sexy all at the same time.

"I suppose we do," I reply.

I don't know what to do. How to handle being around her. I know this attraction I have toward her is totally inappropriate, but I also don't want to be rude.

She looks around like she isn't sure what to do or say next.

My heart is racing at the thought of her ending this conversation and leaving, which makes me blurt out, "I loved your answer the other day. It was pretty clear you know what you're talking about and have a knack for understanding other cultures."

She looks at me with confusion, but at least the panic I was feeling is subsiding.

"Oh, um, I wasn't sure. You kind of ignored my response," she bravely admits.

I rub the back of my neck as tension begins to build. I did do that, but only because I was surprised by her response. It was so thoughtful and spot-on. Brains and beauty are a killer combination, and I wasn't prepared to see she had both in spades.

Instead of giving her the correct response that a professor should have, I panicked and feared that if I did, everyone in the room would see through my feelings.

But I can't tell her that. It would be far too dangerous. Merely being in her presence is already risky enough to my inhibitions, but if she knew the kind of things I had fantasized about...

"I did," I admit without elaborating.

The look on her face is a mix between shock and disappointment. It makes my chest feel weird knowing I put that there.

She nods her head as if she understands what I mean.

"Got it. Well, I'll see you in class on Monday. Have a great weekend, Professor Luke."

She begins to walk away.

Let her do it. Let her walk away.

"Savannah," I shout.

You idiot.

She turns around and the view of her long blonde hair blowing in the wind takes my breath away. I jog the couple steps it takes to catch up with her.

"I'm sorry. I wasn't completely honest with you just now." Her head turns to the side in confusion as she waits for me to go on. "I... I'm just..." *Don't say it.* "I'm attracted to you."

Her eyes are open wide as my words hang in the air. I suddenly feel like a total creep. This older man—her teacher, no less—telling a beautiful young woman he's attracted to her. It's weird.

"I'm so sorry." I fumble over my words as I try to think of a way out of this. "I didn't mean it like that."

"You didn't?" she asks. "How did you mean it?"

"I just, I meant..." I try to think of something, anything that gives me a way out of this. I let out a breath as my shoulders fall down in defeat. "I'm sorry. It's so inappropriate that I said that to you. I just wanted you to understand that I didn't commend your answer because I was afraid... Afraid of your classmates seeing right through my attraction. If I had given you praise that I hadn't given to any other students, or if they noticed the way I look at you... I don't know. But it's obviously inappropriate and nothing would ever happen."

She does the last thing I expect when she starts to laugh.

"Are you laughing at me right now?" I ask, a bit frustrated.

"I'm sorry. I'm not. It's just... I'm attracted to you too. I've been doing everything in my power to squash my little crush."

Fuck me, why does that make my stomach muscles clench with excitement?

"But you're right, it is inappropriate. I have no intentions of acting on it," she says, diverting her gaze toward my to-go coffee cup.

What she's saying is exactly what she needs to. It's responsible, mature, and... it only makes me want her more.

Everything in me wants to pull her body against mine to warm us both up from the frigid cold, to find out what her lips feel like against mine, to bring her to the point where her body is writhing, desperate for me to give her pressure in the one spot that would satisfy her.

Vino and Bailey are sniffing around as they wait patiently for us to pay attention to them. Everything about this feels like a normal interaction between adults, but it isn't. I have to keep reminding myself of that.

I notice her look at my coffee cup again before glancing back up at me.

"But I do hope we can put this aside, because I really want to learn as much as I can from you this semester. Well, not because it's you but because of the subject matter," she clarifies.

"And I want to help you in any way that I can," I tell her. When she looks down at my coffee again, I have to ask. "Do you have a problem with my choice of coffee or something? You keep eyeing my cup. I'm starting to get a little self-conscious."

She laughs, and the sound makes me feel oddly light. I've never experienced that before from something so simple, but it makes me want to do everything in my power to keep making it happen.

"Oh, gosh, no!" she replies. "I can't believe you noticed that. No, it's nothing like that. I've just recently had to cut back on some things to afford this last stretch of school, and coffee from anywhere but my apartment got the axe from my budget. I'm basically just drooling over your coffee."

It's been such a long time since I've struggled with money. To be on such a budget that coffee isn't affordable is foreign to me. To think of Savannah not being able to enjoy such a basic part of one's day makes me irrationally angry.

"Come on." I start to walk as I motion for her to follow.

She looks around like she isn't sure what's happening before her legs move to catch up with me.

"What's going on?" she asks, her voice etched with confusion.

"We're going to go get you some coffee," I tell her as I lead us to the parking lot.

I'm not normally bossy, but I feel this strange need to make this right for her. I can tell she's the type of person to refuse help, to think nobody should do anything for her, and I'm not having it.

"Professor Luke, no! This is insane. I do *not* need coffee."

Yep, I knew she was going to refuse. I lead the way to my car parked in the front, opening the back door to let Vino jump in, and then wait for her dog to get in too.

She stands there holding onto the leash tightly, not making a move to let her dog climb in. Bailey is wagging her tail eagerly as she tries to move forward to join her new buddy in the car.

"Come on, Savannah. It's just a cup of coffee. I won't be able to focus all day if I don't rectify the situation and get you a cup of your favorite coffee. Please, just let me do this. Think of it as a peace offering for both of us since we seem to be attracted to someone who is off limits."

We smile at each other, and after another beat of silence, she finally answers. "Ugh, fine. Go ahead, Bailey." She lets go of the leash, and Bailey all but barrels into the backseat.

I close the door and begin to reach for the passenger door when her hand swats my arm away.

"No! This is not a date. We are friends—or teacher and student—or whatever the hell this is. What it isn't is a date, and men only open doors for dates."

I laugh as I put my hands up in apology. "I'm sorry. I will refrain from all gentlemanly actions if they are so offensive to you," I say with a smile.

She nods her head like she accepts my apology.

"Good," she says as she opens the door herself.

When I walk around the car to get to my side, I can't wipe the smile off my face. She is a piece of work. I love how she went from being shy and timid to telling me like it is within twenty minutes. It's refreshing to be around someone who isn't trying to impress me.

Once you become as successful as I have, women start doing anything they can to get into your orbit, like pretending to be someone they aren't. I know this from experience.

"Okay, pups. Are you ready?" I turn my head and both dogs have their heads smooshed into the black net divider that keeps them from coming to the front of the car.

Me and Savannah both laugh.

"I think they're new BFFs," she jokes.

I pull out of the park and settle into my seat. Every other second, I find my eyes glancing over at the woman who's occupied my thoughts so much these last couple of weeks.

She looks down at the floor of my passenger seat then up at me, her eyes wide in what appears to be disbelief. "Word search!" she shouts. "Oh my gosh! You're an avid word-searcher too?"

I have probably ten word search books down there. It's been one of my favorite stress-relievers since I was a kid. I used to do them all the time with my grandma.

"You like them too?" I ask her.

"Are you kidding me? I'm probably the best out there. I could do them for hours."

She is definitely not who I was expecting her to be. What college student in today's world is obsessed with word games?

"I'm sorry, Savannah, but there's no way you're better than me," I say, defending myself.

She laughs as I park my car in front of the coffee shop, opting to leave the car running for the dogs.

"This spot is visible from inside the building so we can keep our eyes on these guys," I say to her.

She nods and follows me in. We step into the line, and when I look over at her, she's taking a deep breath as she gets a scent of the coffee aroma floating through the air.

God, she's beautiful.

"What's your drink of choice?" I lean into her and get hit with another trace of that mystifying scent.

I can't tell whether it's her or the heat of the building that's warming my insides. I fear it's the first one, which has me on edge.

"I think I'm going to go for the blonde vanilla latte," she tells me.

I give the barista her order, asking for it in the largest size they have. When I look to my left, I see the gift card display and act on instinct.

"I'd also like to purchase a gift card," I tell her.

"Absolutely, sir. How much would you like on it?" she asks.

"Five hundred, please."

"Okay..." she drawls out, clearly not used to getting requests in such large amounts. She works to ring my order up and then says, "That brings your total to five hundred eight dollars and fifty-three cents."

I hand the barista my card and steal a glance at Savannah whose eyes are opened wide in shock. She looks quickly away from me like she caught me doing something wrong. She obviously has no idea I got this for her.

We move to the end of the counter as we wait for Savannah's drink which is ready quickly. She takes it from the barista and smiles warmly at her.

When we get back in the car, she takes a big sip and closes her eyes as she moans over her cup.

Fuck, I adjust myself in my seat. It's like every damn thing this woman does makes my body come to life. I feel like I'm sixteen again and can't help but get hard from the slightest thing she does.

I pull the gift card out of my wallet and hand it to her.

"What's this?" she asks.

"I got it for you."

She sits up straight and looks down at the card in my hand.

"You got that *five hundred dollar* gift card for *me*?" she asks, sounding almost offended.

I don't want her spending the last semester of her senior year drinking cheap-ass crap that she makes at her apartment. It doesn't sit right with me when I know five hundred dollars is nothing more than a simple fix to me.

"Of course. I want you to be well-caffeinated to sit through my boring lectures." I extend my hand further for her to take the card, but she makes no move to meet me in the middle.

"Savannah. Take. The. Card. If you don't, I'm going to stalk you on campus and buy your coffee every morning."

"This is too much," she says while reluctantly grabbing the card.

"I may not know much about you, Savannah, but I can tell that this is not enough for someone like you. Please, just take it, and let's move on."

She takes it and tucks it into her pocket as she whispers, "Thank you."

I know I should get her back to her car and move on with my day, but I don't. There's something about being in her presence that's calming, and I'm not ready to give that up just yet.

"Tell me about yourself," I ask, desperate to know more about her.

She looks at me as she takes another sip of her coffee, and I notice just how green her eyes are. They're so alluring I have trouble focusing on her words.

It looks like she's pondering my question. "I'm from Cincinnati. My dad raised me on his own after my mom passed away when I was little. I'm an only child—well, I was until recently when my dad remarried. Now I have a stepbrother and stepsister from that marriage, but they're in elementary school, so we aren't that close. Um, I love to read, run, and cook."

"How old were you when your mom passed?" I ask, surprised that life has already been so unkind to her. I knew I sensed that she was more mature, more deep than most women I've met. That tends to happen when you're thrown into difficult situations in life.

"I was three. Cancer."

"I'm sorry."

She nods her head like those words mean nothing after she's heard them so many times before.

"How did you pick your major?"

"I heard they had hot professors in the department."

I can't help but let out a huge laugh at that, shaking my head at her joke.

"I'm kidding." She nudges my arm playfully. "I always loved reading growing up. It was a quiet household with just me and my dad. When I was thrust into these worlds within my books, it just sparked this desire to travel and go to these places I was reading about. It always sounded so... magical. And you know, business is always a solid degree to have. So, I tried to combine my dream with being practical, and voila: Marketing and International Business."

"Sounds like you made the right choice."

"I think so."

"How old are you?" I ask because I have to know. Nothing about this interaction feels like talking to a young college student.

"Twenty-two." She looks at me, and her eyes scan my body. It's unnerving because I can see those green eyes appreciating what she sees. If only she knew what I would do to her if I could. "How old are you?"

"Thirty-four."

When our eyes meet, the electricity between us could power a city on its own.

"Twelve years," she whispers before biting her lip.

I suppress the groan that comes up as I focus on her mouth, wondering what it would feel like on mine. What it would feel like wrapped around my dick. Shaking my head, I peel my eyes away and face forward again.

"Twelve years is a lot," I say in an effort to remind myself how wrong these feelings are.

She looks at me inquisitively. "It's not *that* much."

I rest my head on the back of my seat and turn my head toward her. "It's a lot. I need it to be a lot. I need as many reasons as possible to remind myself why this attraction to you is wrong."

I think she senses how serious I am, just how much I need this for my wavering self-control.

"Fine. It's a lot. It's disgusting. You're like a grandpa to me. Take me back to my car, old man. I need to go hang out with people my own age who don't bore me to death."

She mimics my position in the car as her head falls back, and we smile at each other. I know what she's trying to do, but dammit, it's not working like it should. It just makes me adore her more.

"Nice try, but you're not a great actress."

"I'm trying," she breathes.

I nod my head, understanding that I need to be the adult here and end this before we go too far. I put my car into reverse and make myself focus on the road ahead instead of the beautiful woman next to me.

Chapter Five

Savannah

I'm sitting on Tricia's bed, only halfway listening as she rambles on about this new guy she's been talking to. I'm struggling to absorb anything that she's saying because I can't stop replaying my afternoon with Luke on Saturday.

On one hand, it was nice to be open about how attracted I am to him and to know my feelings are reciprocated. On the other hand, we both know we can't act on it, and I have no clue where that leaves us.

Clearly not updated on the forbidden nature of it all, my stomach is all messed up with excitement knowing class starts in less than an hour.

Ugh, if he wears his slacks and button-down shirt with the sleeves rolled up again, I'm screwed. How am I expected to focus when his insanely sexy forearms are on display like that?

I can see it now. Me begging the university for a break on my failing grade.

"Please give me a break, I just couldn't focus."

"Why couldn't you focus, Miss Davis?" they'd ask.

"Well, you see, my professor's forearms were showing. They were so muscular and veiny that I kept fantasizing about what they

would look like trailing all over my body or flexing while his hand pumped his dick."

Yeah, I don't see that going over well.

"Let's go bitches. Time for class," Shannon says as she pops her head into the room.

The four of us grab our things and start the walk to the building in the freezing weather. I keep my head down to avoid it getting hit by the wind.

It's colder than usual out today, the lake effect weather making the wind so cold it stings your face as it whips through.

Even though it's not a long walk to class, we're walking past the coffee shop when Shannon speaks up.

"Ahh, I'm frickin' colder than a penguin's pecker. Let's run into the coffee shop real quick. I need something to warm me up in class."

"Where the hell do you come up with this shit?" Aubrey laughs as we speed walk our way to the coffee shop.

And that's how I end up walking into class with my favorite latte in hand—my second cup of the day. We take a seat in the front to help with my worsening vision. If I sit in the back, I can't read the projector screen very easily. Glasses are on my list of things to get as soon as I get a real job with real benefits.

Luke is standing in the corner, back to the crowd, as he talks with the TA. Rebecca is laughing at something he's said, and if you ask me, she's laughing a little too hard.

Almost as if he senses me staring, he turns around and his eyes land directly on mine. My heart flutters and my body feels lighter just by having his attention. He glances down at my coffee cup and it's impossible not to notice the way one corner of his mouth lifts up.

I can't help but smile back and lift my cup in the air, making him shake his head with a grin. Coming back to reality, we both realize we could be causing a scene and immediately shift our gazes apart and put our focus on the class ahead of us.

I'm hooked by his charisma throughout the entire lecture as I watch him move across the room, speaking animatedly.

"You see," he begins, "business outside of America, it's about the *people*." He points down at a student in the front row and engages them. "If I were trying to do business with you, and you lived in Germany, I would try to find out more about *you*. I would want to know how our personalities work together, what about us is similar and shows that we will make a good fit."

He smiles as he appears to recall something. "I've had a couple of times where I've been to Europe and I could tell instantly, there wasn't a connection between the potential client and myself. It's a drastic difference from how it goes down here in America. It's more...dare I say...romantic."

It's clear he has a passion for the work that he does. The way he speaks of the subject keeps you captivated the entire time.

When the lecture is over, I sit in my seat and slowly pack my things. Even though I've been near him for ninety-minutes, it did nothing to scratch the itch to see him. It was too impersonal. I want to talk to him again. Learn more about him.

You want to do a lot more than that with him.

Nope, that's not true. It can't be true. If I want to learn more about him, it's nothing more than just as a friend. *Friends.* I just need to keep reminding myself of that.

Shit, I'm all over the place.

"Hey, you coming?" Tricia asks.

"I—um," I stutter, pretending to dig through my bag. "You guys go ahead. I'm heading home right now. I just need to find my gloves."

"Cool. I'll see you Wednesday," she replies before catching up with the girls.

I look down and see the gloves were in my hand the entire time. Smirking to myself at what a weak attempt at lying that was, I can only hope she didn't notice.

I close my laptop and put it back in my bag. The rest of the class has filtered out, leaving only me, Luke, and Rebecca.

She has half her ass propped up on his desk in the front of the room while he packs up. She clearly has no clue I'm even in the room while she flirts with him.

I make a mental note to dig into the university rules to find out if teaching assistants are allowed to date professors. Scratch that; that's really messed up that I want to take it that far.

"I can't imagine what it's like to travel the world tasting wine," she says with a sigh. "I would love to try some of your favorites. I'm a huge wine drinker."

I want to roll my eyes but his eyes meet mine, and I forget about everything when he looks at me.

He looks back at Rebecca. "Uh, sure. I can make a list for you."

"I'm such a spazz, though, when it comes to understanding the complexities of the wine. Maybe you can teach me."

Oh, God. I'm not coming across as that desperate, am I?

You just lied to your best friends so you can stay after and do the same thing.

The thought alone makes me grab my bag and walk quickly up the steps of the auditorium until I'm outside. The cold air hits my lungs, and I let my head fall back as I look up at the gray winter sky.

What the hell am I thinking?

I can't believe I'm so naïve to think he has any interest in forming a real friendship. Not to mention it'd be foolish for both of us to think we can admit we're attracted to each other and not let anything happen.

I want to go home right now, but I have to make a stop at the library to grab a book for my other international business class. The walk from this building is only about five minutes, but that feels like an hour in this temperature.

I put on my cream hat and gloves, then begin to make my way.

I wonder what Luke thinks about me. Does he think I'm some pathetic, lovesick student who wants attention and waits after class for him?

More importantly, maybe I should ask myself if I am a pathetic, lovesick student.

I'd be lying if I said my crush is gone, but I really feel a magnetic pull to him. It's almost like my brain has no real say in the matter as my body takes over.

He looked so handsome tonight in his blue slacks and crisp white dress shirt. Like the universe wanted to torture me, he rolled his shirtsleeves up to just below his elbows halfway through the lecture.

When I walk into the library, I'm momentarily surprised by how vacant it is, but then I remember it's the coldest month of the year. Nobody wants to be outside of their home for longer than necessary.

I take the main steps up the stairs and turn right. I've been to this area of the library enough times before to know exactly where the section I need is. I have to write a report on the impact of global corporations on the economy, and I just need to pick up a few books to cite in my essay.

The further down the hall I get, the less people there are, until eventually, I feel like I'm the only one here. It's kind of a creepy feeling. It makes me feel like I'm in a Scream movie, and the killer is going to jump out with a knife.

Okay, I just need to focus on the task at hand and not think about getting stabbed to death by a fictional movie character.

I pull out a couple of books on my topic and start to skim the contents, trying to decide if they're worthy of being cited or not.

It's been about ten minutes and I've already found a few good books that I think I could use. I turn around and scream when I see a male figure leaning against the books.

"Shh. Calm down. It's just me," Luke says with a concerned look. "I'm sorry, I didn't mean to scare you."

"I thought you were the Ghostface Killer," I say without thinking.

His mouth turns up. "Who the hell is the Ghostface Killer?"

"You know... the killer from the Scream movies," I say with my hand still held over my racing heart.

"Why, or maybe how is a better question, would I be the killer from a film?"

"Because I was just thinking about how being back here alone made me feel creeped out. That made me think of the Ghostface Killer, and next thing I know, I turn around and you're standing there."

"Ahh, makes total sense now." He folds his arms across his chest, now leaning against the stacks with his shoulder. He looks every bit the sexy professor type you would picture from the movies.

"What are you doing here?" I try to deflect from my embarrassing admission.

"Just came here to find something for my lecture on Wednesday." His eyes skim from my boots to my face with a look of amusement and I shiver under his attention. "Was there something you needed after class Savannah?"

"Uh, no. I was just a little slow getting my stuff together. I couldn't find my gloves."

I can tell he sees right through my lie. He bites his lip, but a smile still breaks through. His head leans to the side as if he's trying to read my thoughts.

"Are you sure? It seemed like you were ready. Your things were packed," he says as his eyebrows raise.

I fold my arms across my chest in defense. "What exactly are you implying?"

"I'm saying maybe you were waiting to talk to me. Maybe you noticed how hard I was trying to not look at your beautiful face during class, and you wanted to yell at me for failing so miserably."

It feels like my heart actually skips a beat. I try to act not affected by his words, but it's impossible.

"I don't think friends say things like that to each other," I say breathily.

He pushes off the books and takes a step closer to me. One smell of his woodsy cologne and I feel like my brain has lost all ability to make rational decisions. I instinctually take a step toward him until we are only a foot apart.

The air around us feels charged.

"I'm new to this being friends with someone I'm attracted to thing," he says. "Like right now, I know what's happening is dangerous, meaning I should back away."

He stands in front of me, making no move to put distance between us. His chest is rising and falling in rapid succession like mine.

"But..." I begin.

"But my body doesn't seem to want to obey what my brain is screaming for me to do," he finishes.

I picture Rebecca standing in front of his desk, making him smile, and I feel the jealousy back in full force.

"She wants you," I say to him.

He looks confused. "Who does?"

"Rebecca," I admit.

He tucks my hair behind my ear. A subtle gesture that I feel deep in my bones.

"Does that make you jealous?" he asks.

"It shouldn't."

"Answer my question, Savannah," he demands.

"Fine." I throw my hands up, knowing he can see the truth anyway. "It made me jealous."

That makes him smile. "Good."

"Good?" I ask with frustration. "Why is that good?"

"Because I have to watch college guys come up to you at bars, in class, in the coffee shop, everywhere you go... It wouldn't be fair if I was the only one going crazy."

"You get jealous?" my voice raises with hope.

I shouldn't like that, it shouldn't fill me with happiness, but it does. Everything in me is thrilled that he gets green with envy when a guy comes up to me. I should tell him all of them are just friends, but I don't.

"I shouldn't," he whispers.

His lips are inches from mine, so close I can taste the minty scent of his breath. Remembering the million reasons why this is a bad idea feels impossible at the moment. All I can think about is how good it would feel to give in, to fuse my lips to his and melt into him.

There seems to be something beyond my control pushing our bodies together. When our lips are just about to touch, the sound of footsteps approaching makes us speedily step away from each other.

He starts to massage the back of his neck while he looks down at the ground.

"Shit, I'm sorry. I can't believe I almost did that," he says while reluctantly meeting my eyes.

My breaths are still coming quickly, now with fear mixed in as I hear the stranger in the aisle next to us.

"It's okay. I obviously wasn't doing anything to stop it. Don't worry, it won't happen again."

"Right. Look, I should go," he mutters as he backs away from me.

"But what about that book you needed?" I ask.

He continues to put distance between the two of us. The air starts to feel colder as the distance grows. I wrap my arms around myself, trying anything to ease the chill.

"I'll get it another time. I'll see you in class, Savannah. Good-night." He spins around and rounds the bookcase, out of sight within seconds.

My head falls back as I look up at the cheap florescent lights. I almost kissed my professor... Or my professor almost kissed me. Either way, I can't believe that just happened.

Chapter Six

Luke

It's been three weeks since I almost kissed Savannah. I was *this* close to kissing those pouty lips of hers, and I would have done it if we weren't interrupted. I was too caught up in the moment, in how she made me feel, to stop myself.

Never in my life would I believe I was the type of guy who would end up in this situation. I'm the good one. I've always strived to do what's right, no matter how much I want something. Maybe I'm not the stand-up guy I thought I was.

That's why I've kept my distance ever since. When class is over, I pack up my things in record time and am out the door along with the students.

The good news is that Rebecca has no time to hang around my desk either. Two birds, one stone.

The bad news is that I miss Savannah.

Is it even possible to miss someone you barely know? The chemistry is still there between us, floating around the room during every class while I do everything in my power to focus on my lecture.

"Lucas!" my brother Marcus shouts. "Snap out of it."

I look around the dinner table at my parents' house, realizing all eyes are on me.

"Huh? I'm sorry, I was just... thinking about something," I answer back vaguely.

"Yeah, we got that, buddy. What's up with you lately? You've been distracted the last couple weeks," he responds.

Ma gives me a worried stare. "It's because he's taken on too much," she says. "Are you okay, Lucas?"

"I'm fine. Nothing to worry about over here. I was literally just lost in thought. I'm not having some kind of mental breakdown or anything."

"Uncle Lucas, what's a mental breakdown?" my six-year-old niece Sienna asks.

"That's nothing you need to be concerned with at your age, sweetie," my brother Gabe, her father, responds.

It's nice to be close with your family, but sometimes that means you can't hide much from them. Mia is eyeing me inquisitively. I know she isn't buying it, but thankfully she doesn't speak up. Women are so intuitive, and Mia is no exception.

"So, what kind of wine are we trying tonight?" Pa asks, changing the subject with a subtle wink in my direction.

The bottle that Gabe is opening is the new Chianti Classico that we found at a little vineyard in Panzano, Italy. There aren't many bottles in production yet, making it a rare and expensive find.

"Are you sure we should be drinking a Panzano wine? We aren't exactly stocked with an unlimited supply of them," Marcus says.

Gabe looks down at Alexis, his girlfriend, and smiles.

"It's a special occasion," Gabe says as he goes around the table to fill everybody's glass.

When he gets back to his seat, he grabs Alexis's hand.

"What's up?" Mia asks.

"Everybody, Alexis and I have an announcement." Ma and Mia gasp at the table then wait with bated breath for Gabe to continue. "Alexis and I are getting married," he finally finishes.

The table erupts with joy. Ma is immediately crying, Pa stands up to shake Gabe's hand, and Mia jumps on top of Alexis as she screams in her ear.

"Alex is going to be my mommy!" Sienna screams.

I grab my niece and give her a big squeeze. "Yes, she is, squirt," I tell her.

The rest of dinner is filled with discussions of wedding dates and dress shopping, and any other intrusive questions my family can come up with. Alexis doesn't have the most supportive family, so she's always said she loves how close we are. I wonder if she's reconsidering her words yet.

But when I look at her, I see a smile that is extending from ear to ear, making it clear that she couldn't be happier.

"How about everyone retires to the family room and I'll get to work on the dishes," Ma suggests as she begins to clear the table.

"I'll help you, Ma," Mia says.

The rest of us take our wine to the couch and get comfortable in front of the fireplace. I notice Gabe and Alexis holding hands as they walk.

"Alex, are you sure you want to spend the rest of your life with Mr. Grumpy?" Marcus jokes, winking at her.

Marcus likes to ruffle Gabe's feathers, and he's damn good at it.

"At least he's getting married," Pa quips.

"Why are you taking his side?" Marcus asks.

"I'll take your side when you start giving me grandkids. I'm not getting any younger."

I laugh at their banter, proving to them that I'm paying attention now, but inside, I get this strange feeling of jealousy.

For years, I've enjoyed the single life. As I approached my thirties, when you would think I'd be ready to settle down, our business took off. I was thrown into money, power, and beautiful foreign women.

It wasn't until these last few months that I started to lose interest, craving something deeper and more meaningful.

"That's it for tonight. Don't forget that you have a test on Monday on the material we discussed this week. Have a great weekend," I say, dismissing the class.

I look over at Savannah and notice her laughing at something her friend said. Her signature grin is lighting up her face, and I can't help but think that she's so damn beautiful. I thought that as the semester continued, my attraction would fade, but that hasn't been the case.

I throw my materials into my briefcase and start up the stairs to get away from temptation. I know it's late, but I feel like I need a cup of coffee to get through the rest of the evening. It's been another twelve-hour workday for me, and the long weeks and even longer days are starting to catch up with me.

My legs move quickly toward the shop with a second motivation for the coffee now: warmth.

I open the doors and am hit with the familiar aroma of mixed coffee grounds. The night crowd of college students has begun to fill the seats as they desperately try to stay awake for all-nighters and last-minute cramming.

Even with how busy they are, it doesn't take longer than five minutes for me to stand in line and get my coffee. I take a couple of sips by the door to warm myself up, then push it open, braving the nighttime winter breeze.

As I'm approaching my car in the parking lot, I'm distracted by the sound of bickering coming from a familiar voice.

"Just leave me alone, Miles," she says.

A couple of cars down from mine stands Savannah and the douche from the bar who had his hands on her. I can't believe I'm witnessing her trying to get away from him for the second time.

I take rapid steps toward the two, trying to calm myself down on the way.

"Hey!" I shout, making both of them jump. "A woman says *leave me alone*, you leave her alone. Why the hell am I having to repeat myself to you?"

"Who the hell are you?" he snaps back.

"Miles, just leave it alone." Savannah stands between us as I move in closer.

"No, I don't know who this asshole thinks he is talking to me like that. I've never even met you," Miles argues.

"That's where you're wrong. Obviously, you were too drunk at the bar the first—and what should have been the last—time you had your hands on Savannah. You wouldn't let go then, either. So, unless you want me turning you in to the police, I'd suggest you listen to the girl and leave her alone."

He throws his hands up in defeat. "Whatever, man. She isn't worth it," he says, then spins on his heel and takes off.

I look down at Savannah as she hugs herself. My fists clench, aching to wrap her in my arms and tell her I won't let anything happen to her.

"I'm sorry, Luke. I can't believe you had to step in again." She looks down at the ground, appearing self-conscious.

"Who is that guy?" I demand.

She looks up at me. "Oh, uh, he's my ex. We dated for a couple months last semester."

"Has he ever hurt you, Savannah?" I struggle to get the words out, fearing the answer.

Her eyes open wide in surprise. "No, no, of course not. Actually, this is a side of him I've never seen before."

"I don't like the idea of you walking alone on campus at night," I tell her honestly, omitting the fact that it literally makes my stomach churn thinking about anything happening to her.

"It's okay. I don't think he would actually do anything. Plus, I don't really have much of a choice. I've gotta go to class," she says with a smile.

"Here." I reach my hand out before I can stop myself. "Give me your phone."

She looks puzzled as she grabs her phone out of her coat pocket and extends it toward me.

"Can you get into your contacts first?" I add before taking the phone from her.

"What're you doing?"

"I'm giving you my phone number. I don't live far from campus. If anything happens that scares you or makes you feel uncomfortable, I want you to run into the nearest building and call me. I'll walk with you to your car." I start to type my information into her phone.

"You don't have to do that," she begins to argue, but I put my hand up.

"Please, Savannah. We're talking about your safety here. It's not a big deal to reach out to someone for help once in a while. Promise me you will use it if you need to."

She sighs. "I promise. Thank you for being so nice. Between this and the gift card, I don't know how to repay you."

"Your safety is payment enough for me."

She rolls her eyes. "You're not making it easy to find you any less attractive."

I laugh. "I'll text you a list of all my unappealing qualities."

"That would be much appreciated."

We both stand in comfortable silence while we smile at each other. I know the next person to speak is going to have to put an end to this, which is why I let the moment continue.

Savannah shrugs her shoulders. "Well, I should get going. Thanks again for everything. I'll see you on Monday."

"Goodnight, Savannah. Be safe."

She nods her head and then gets in her car. I stand stuck in my spot as I watch her pull out and drive away, the cold weather momentarily forgotten. As soon as I come to, I make the short trek back to my car and hop in. Somehow, my coffee is still warm. All of that happened in the span of minutes, but any time I spend with Savannah feels like the world comes to a stop.

On the drive home, my thoughts drift to images of her. She has occupied much of my thoughts since the moment I met her, and the distance I've tried to put between the two of us doesn't seem to have diminished anything I'm feeling.

A twelve-year age difference isn't that much, right? I mean, Alexis and Gabe are fourteen years apart, and neither I nor anyone in our family ever blinked an eye at their relationship.

If I just manage to keep my distance until the semester is over, maybe I can consider asking her out. She'll be graduated, and I'll likely be done with my time as an adjunct at the school. I just need to keep our relationship strictly professional until then.

I can do that... can't I?

Chapter Seven

Savannah

"Come on, Bailey," I whisper in the cold, dark night. "Hurry up and go potty."

Bailey sniffs around the small grass patch on the sidewalk, seeming unhappy with her only choice of grass to pee on. I'm right outside my sketchy apartment building but refuse to walk any further away at this time of night.

"Hey, pretty," a male says from behind me.

The tall figure heads toward me with a friend by his side. I shift indignantly from foot to foot.

"What's someone as pretty as you doing out here alone?" he says with a twisted smile.

I'm usually a good judge of character by first impression, and my gut is telling me these two are trouble. Their gazes hold nothing in them. The most dangerous and scary kind of eyes are one's that look like they've lost their soul and ability to feel even the tiniest bit of remorse.

I try to step away but find myself backed up against a tree. My body begins to tremble as images of all the things they could intend to do flood my brain.

"What do you want?" I ask with a shaky voice.

They continue toward me, lips turned up. "That's a loaded question, honey. I'd say at the moment... you," he growls.

I want to scream for help, but it's like one of those nightmares you have when your voice won't work. I'm paralyzed in fear. They take another step until they're only inches away. Just as one of them reaches for me, Bailey jumps in front of me ferociously. She growls louder and more intimidatingly than I've ever heard from her. The two guys start to back away. Not satisfied with their distance, Bailey makes another sudden move in their direction, and they take off running.

Tears begin to fall down my cheeks as I lay my head against the tree. I think I was just seconds away from the worst moment of my life, from possibly the *last* moment of my life. The trembling in my body shows no signs of slowing down.

I need to get inside, knowing I can't be out here by myself for another second. Bailey begins to tug at her leash as she leads me, like she knows she needs to get me to the safety of the building. Despite my wobbly legs, I take the entryway steps two at a time and slam the door behind me. I go through making sure I've locked all the locks on my door, then take off for my bed.

As soon as I get in, I pull my white down comforter over me. Bailey is up on my bed and snuggled by my side, wrapped in my arms.

"You saved my life, Bailey," I cry. "Thank you."

She rewards me with a kiss on the nose before putting her head down and going to sleep.

Way too wound up to rest, I pick my phone up off the nightstand and start to scroll through social media. It's Friday night, so there are people posting pics of what party they're at. As the night continues, you can see in their eyes that they have consumed more and more alcohol.

I don't know what it is lately, but I've had no interest in being a part of those nights like I used to. Most people are living it up their senior year, and here I am... completely over the whole thing.

I do miss the girls, though. I would be on the couch with their worried eyes on me asking what they could do if this happened in our joint apartment. Although this likely wouldn't have happened in the first place if I still lived with them in the nicer part of town.

One thing is for sure, looking through this stuff is doing nothing to take my mind off what just happened. I look through my apps and still feel unsatisfied with my options. Maybe I can find a new app, like a game.

I scroll through solitaire, spider solitaire, trivia, and more until I come across word search. That's exactly what I need to make my brain focus on something else, even if it's still thinking about other things in the background. At least a part of it will be occupied.

As the app starts to download, I think of Luke and all the crossword puzzles in his car. What are the odds that him and I would both be into them?

It's just my luck to find what seems to be the perfect guy for me, yet he's totally off limits.

The app finishes downloading, so I open it up and scroll through the game options when I come across something I've never seen before.

New feature: Play A Friend.

I sit up at that, Luke immediately coming to mind. I wonder what he's doing right now, if it'd be ridiculous to reach out to him.

He did give me his number this week.

No, I could never text him to play a game with me. He gave me the number for safety purposes and emergencies.

Although, judging by the amount of word search books he had on the floor of his car, he would find this pretty cool. He did also tell me there was no way I match his skills. What better way to find out who's really the superior word search player?

I would normally never consider texting him, but after the night I've had, I don't think I can find it in me to care. Maybe this is exactly what I need to calm these jitters still coursing through my body.

I forward the game in a text to him.

Ten minutes go by without any response, and that's when reality sets in.

I just texted my professor at ten on a Friday night.

What the hell was I thinking? He's not some old, washed-up guy who spends his weekends alone. I bet he's out on a date with some beautiful, sophisticated woman that I would never measure up to. They're probably drinking some fancy bottle of wine in an expensive restaurant, and I just texted him a freakin' word search invite.

Before the embarrassment can completely take over, a beep from my phone pulls me out of my thoughts.

Luke: First of all, I can't believe I never knew this existed. Second, I feel bad that I'm being forced to destroy you.

A smile takes over my face. I can't believe he texted me back, and it wasn't him telling me how inappropriate me reaching out is and how he only gave me the number for emergencies. If only I could tell him this is an emergency. I almost died tonight, and I need him to distract me from that reality. Instead, I opt to pretend like it never happened and be my cheery self.

Me: Sounds like you're living in a fantasy world. Game on.

I click on the link that brings me to our game. The countdown for him to join starts, and I actually squeal when he enters the game only seconds behind me. It looks like we each have our own screen of the same puzzle with individual timers, so whoever finishes first will be declared the winner.

I sit cross-legged on my bed, my heart racing for an entirely different reason from half an hour ago. The timer starts and I'm off. There are twenty words, and the theme is beach. The first word I find is lobster, then before I know it, I'm lost in the game. Only minutes have gone by, but I only have three words left.

It's so scary not knowing where he is on the puzzle. I get to the last word, and I'm about to highlight it when my phone dings.

Sorry, you're too slow!

Ugh, he beat me. I slide the app closed and move to our text strand with a smile on my face. I can just picture him gloating to himself.

Me: Dammit. I was on my last word. I want a rematch.

I refuse to let him show me up, knowing that was just luck for him. There's no way he's faster than me. I've grown up on this shit, I've made word search my bitch.

Luke: Savannah: a sore loser. I expected better from you. Game on, princess.

I go back in the app to find him waiting for me to join. We take off on the next game, sports themed this time. I'm cruising through it, the pressure to win only fueling my competitiveness.

I'm on the final word again which ironically happens to be victory. I swear, if he wins again in the nick of time, I'm gonna chuck something.

Winner! appears on my screen.

Yes, take that, Luke. A text comes in seconds later.

Luke: Nice one, princess. We can't leave it as a tie. Best out of three, loser owes the winner.

Me: Loser owes the winner what exactly?

I really shouldn't care, I'm going to win. His win was clearly just a fluke, I hadn't hit my stride yet.

Luke: Anything. Winner gets to pick anything.

Anything? Okay, I need to think about this first. It's not that I don't have the confidence that I'm going to win, but anything can be.... well, anything. What if it's something humiliating, like standing up in front of the class and singing? Or like something more risqué like... No, don't go there, Savannah.

My stomach does a flutter at the mere thought of him implying something sexual or romantic, but there's no way that's his intention.

Minutes have gone by, and I still haven't answered his challenge. My phone rings and my jaw drops when I see that it's a facetime from *him*!

I sit up straight and look around my room then down at myself. Shit, I'm in an old gray sweater and black pajama pants. My makeup has long been removed, leaving my face bare and my hair up in a ponytail.

Okay, deep breath. *You can do this, Savannah.*

Crap, my nerves are back, but for an entirely different reason.

I answer the call, totally unprepared for the sight of this man. He appears on my screen, and when he sees me, the smile that takes over his face makes my insides turn to mush.

"Wow," he says through his grin. "Do you ever *not* look breath-takingly beautiful?"

My face feels like it's on fire from the compliment. "Stop it, I know I look horrible."

"I don't think I should even go down this road of telling you what your beauty does to me." There's a pause before he contin-ues. "You didn't answer me. I was worried my offer scared you."

I smirk at him then shrug, opting for honesty. "I think I was over-analyzing."

"What were you thinking?" he asks, his face looking like he's equally interested *and* scared of my answer.

He looks so damn adorable and sexy at the same time. It looks like he's lying on his couch, hair all tousled and messy, with a sweatshirt on to complete the laidback look.

Clearly, no matter what this man wears, he looks like he should be in front of a camera. If I were the photographer, I would do everything in my power to get him to take his clothes off.

I don't know why I feel so shy, so exposed in front of him, but I shrug my shoulders again. "At first, I thought you'd make me stand in front of the class and embarrass myself by singing or something," I admit. His loud laugh makes me feel more compelled to admit the full truth to him. "Then I started to wonder if it would be more... sexual."

His smile disappears, immediately replaced with a carnal look.

"What would you think if it did turn sexual?" he asks, voice hoarse like he could barely get the words out.

This is dangerous territory. We can't seem to be around each other without things heading in this direction.

"I don't think I should answer that," I whisper, like someone might hear the naughty thoughts circling around my brain.

He growls. No fucking joke. I actually *see* his Adam's apple vibrate with the hum of his growl. If I wasn't wet before, I am now.

"Savannah, we shouldn't be doing any of this. We're well past the line of professor and student, and yet I can't seem to pump the brakes. At least if it's on the phone, we can't cross the point of no return."

"Are you saying... you want to know what I was thinking you might make me do?" I ask, as I feel my adventurous side push through.

"Princess, I *need* to know," he says, his eyes growing even more dark and dangerous.

What is it with this man versus the college guys I've been with? Everything he says makes my body heat up, subconsciously responding to his every word, his every move.

Even when he doesn't say anything, the looks he gives are so damn confident, and yet they never cross the line to cocky. It's like he knows what he has in front of him and is in awe, but he isn't desperate for it.

Whenever I've been with a college guy, I can feel how desperate they are to impress me—or worse, to get me in bed.

"It started out innocent, with just you asking me to kiss you. But that wasn't enough," I say. He doesn't make a move to rush me or ask me to go on. He just lies there watching... waiting. My breathing becomes erratic like I just got done running, which makes no sense considering I'm lying in bed. "Then you asked—no, demanded that I get on my knees."

I'm not sure if I should keep going. It's clear as day where I'm going with this, but I'm not sure if we're having phone sex right now.

"Fuck, princess. I'm hard as a rock right now," he groans, reaching down and readjusting himself. "I know even saying that is crossing another line, but shit, hearing you say those words..."

"I did it," I decide to continue. "I obeyed your command."

Before he can respond, a look of confusion passes over his face, followed by his hand rubbing his face while he moans in frustration.

"My ma's calling me right now. Shit, I should take this. Raincheck on the tiebreaker, Princess?" he asks.

"Yeah," I reply, hoping my disappointment isn't obvious. "Raincheck."

"Goodnight, Savannah."

I smile. "Goodnight."

Chapter Eight

Luke

Standing in the shower, I look down at my erection which hasn't fully gone away, even with that bucket of ice dropped on me when my mother called.

We were definitely going to have phone sex if we weren't interrupted. Shit, I had just moved my hand down to grip my throbbing cock.

Hearing her say those words to me, looking a mix between shy and daring—it was too much.

It was nice hearing from her tonight, but I was surprised by her boldness. I was already lying on the couch thinking of her, as I often do these days, and it felt good to know she was doing the same. Well, not good, because that would be inappropriate, but...

Oh, fuck it, we're so far past inappropriate now.

Which makes me think that maybe we can do it again. Just that, the talking on the phone. If I know from the beginning that we're going to talk, just talk, I might be able to keep it in safe territory.

For now, if I can just give my body a little glimpse of what it wants—a fantasy of the woman I've been craving for weeks.

My head falls forward, letting the warm water hit the back of my neck. With one hand on the wall holding the weight of my body, I close my eyes and let instinct take over.

Savannah's sitting in the front row of my class. It's summertime, and she's in a tight pink dress. She isn't wearing a bra, the air conditioning is running full-blast, and her nipples are poking through the thin material, teasing me.

My hand wraps tightly around my dick and begins to pump up and down, slowly at first. My body wants the release, but my brain wants to draw out the fantasy.

I keep talking to the class, explaining what their next assignment is going to be, but Savannah knows my eyes are on her. She leans back in her chair. At first, I'm deflated, thinking she's going to start taking notes, that she isn't in on this little game that I thought we were playing.

Then she opens her legs a little farther. She brings her pencil to her mouth and starts dragging it slowly around her lips.

I try to lean a bit to my right to catch a glimpse of her panties. Dammit! I can't see from this angle.

My hand is starting to pump harder as the anticipation grows.

Fuck, I want to see her panties. What color are they? Just the thought has pre-cum leaking out of my tip. Dammit, Savannah. Open those sexy little legs, I need to see.

Instead of waiting any longer, I move to the end of my desk with my pen in hand. I open my fingers just enough for the pen to drop to the floor.

I slowly squat down and extend my arm out for the pen. As I look up to her seat in the front row, I'm greeted with a bare pink pussy under her dress. She isn't wearing any underwear, and she wants me to know it. Her sultry smile confirms that. I feel saliva pool in my mouth at the sight. She's glistening down there, wet from the enjoyment of being naughty and showing her professor her beautiful cunt.

I stand up quickly and shout, "Class dismissed!"

I don't care if it's early, I need everybody out immediately. The students file out without even questioning me, but my little princess is sitting there in her seat, waiting patiently.

Once the room is empty, I walk back to my desk.

"Miss Davis, a word?" I growl.

She stands up and walks slowly over to my desk. "Yes, Professor Luke?"

"It appears that you forgot something when you were getting ready this morning," I inquire.

With her arms behind her back, she sways back and forth innocently. "Oh, silly me. I hope I didn't offend you."

That's about all the restraint I have. I advance on her, wrap an arm around her waist, and use my free hand to run my fingers slowly up her thigh. She sucks in a breath while her jaw falls slack. She wants this just as much as I do.

"Do you need some help, princess? I noticed how wet you are down there. It must be so uncomfortable."

"Please," she begs.

That's all I need. My hand moves under her dress until my fingers are greeted with the slick evidence of her arousal. She whimpers as soon as my fingers hit her clit.

"That's it, baby. Just let me take care of you," I whisper.

I work in slow circles around her clit. When I feel like she's ready, I slide them into her pussy as my thumb moves to keep attention on her clit. She's a mess of sounds and breaths as I work my hand expertly.

"Fuck, Professor Luke. I'm coming!" she screams.

I growl in frustration as my fist squeezes and my balls tighten. Thick ropes of cum pump out of me, landing on the floor of my shower. Once I've worked out my release, I rest my forehead on the wall.

Shit! All that fantasy did was make me want the real thing even more.

I'm so fucked.

I finish cleaning up and aggressively rip my towel off the bar. I'm so damn angry at myself for not being able to get ahold of these feelings. This is not who I am. I'm not the type of man that gets caught up in such an inappropriate situation.

I need a glass of wine, maybe something from the south of France this time. Madiran sounds just right. I open the bottle and pour myself a glass, watching as Vino follows me to the couch. As soon as I sit down, she joins me and then rests her head on my leg.

I take a sip and let the fruity notes settle on my tongue before swallowing. There's something in the process of drinking wine that is so relaxing. It's not the alcohol that does it; it's the fact that you have to use all of your senses to really take in the entirety of the wine, leaving no room for your brain to focus on anything but the wine. It always puts me fully present in the moment, and not in my worries or troubles.

My phone, which is sitting on the coffee table, begins to light up and vibrate on the wood.

I lean forward and swipe it off the table. It's my brother, Gabe.

"Hello?" I answer.

"Hey, man. I figured I'd get your voicemail on a Friday night."

"Then why'd you call if you thought I wouldn't answer?" I ask.

"I've got some news. It's kind of urgent," he says.

"Oh, yeah? Everything all right, man?"

I sit up straight, hoping Sienna is okay. That little squirt is our family's pride and joy. Her smile is enough to make any bad mood lift, even just a little.

"It's more than alright. I just wanted to let you know that the wedding is gonna be a little sooner than expected. Alexis and I want to get started on expanding our family sooner rather than later since I'm not gettin' any younger."

A small laugh reverberates through my chest. "Don't remind me. That means I'm gettin' old too. So, when's the big day?"

"Two weeks," he answers.

I choke on the wine I had just taken a sip of. After I get done with my coughing fit, all the while hearing Gabe chuckling in the background, I put my glass down.

"Two weeks? How do you even plan a wedding in two weeks?" I question.

"Easy, you tell Ma she'll get more grandbabies sooner. Her and Alexis have been running around town putting everything together. The good news is that it's the coldest month of the year. Nobody wants to get married in Cleveland in February. So, we can pick basically wherever we want."

"Damn. Okay, well, good thing I'm in town in two weeks."

"I checked our calendar at work already. All four of us are scheduled to be in town. Listen, Alexis and I want something small. We're gonna forgo most of the classic wedding traditions and make it simple. There won't be any wedding party, so I hope you and Marcus aren't offended that there won't be speeches or groomsmen."

Gabe's already done the big wedding, and things didn't exactly work out for him. Angie ended up ditching her husband and daughter for a more "glamorous" life in California. It makes perfect sense that he has no interest in making a show of it this time around. This is about the real love shared between him and Alexis.

"I get it, man. It's all about what you two want. I'm just happy you finally found the woman who deserves you and Sienna."

"Nah, you got it backward. Alexis deserves better than me, but I'll spend the rest of my life trying to be the best man I can for her."

I hear weird noises followed by giggling in the background. "What's going on? Is that Alex?"

"You're asking for it, babe. Get your ass in the bedroom. Ugh, hey, I gotta go. I'll be in touch with more details."

"You guys are gross. I'm not an idiot, go have sex with your fiancé. Congrats, man. Can't wait to celebrate," I tell him before hanging up.

My brother is getting married in two weeks.

There was a day I thought he was so broken that he'd never trust another woman again. It takes a toll on a man when his wife leaves not only him but their baby girl too. He thought if he were just a better man, a better husband, Angie never would have left.

Turns out, Angie had no business becoming a mother in this world. She was too selfish and self-centered. But thank God she did because I couldn't imagine our family without Sienna.

Chapter Nine

Savannah

I've been dying for the weekend to be over so I can see Professor Luke again. Things got cut short on Friday, and now I have no idea how to act around him.

I'm so hard right now played on repeat in my mind.

I've never had phone sex before. I had no idea how hot it was to be so close to someone and yet so far away. To feel like they were touching you when they weren't even in the room.

Now here he is, lecturing to our class like it never happened. Well, I don't know if that's true. I have no idea what's going on in his head, but I'm afraid his mother wasn't even calling that night. What if he panicked and wanted it to end but didn't want to hurt my feelings?

"Just a reminder. This Friday is your written exam on International Business case studies. You will have the entire length of the class to complete it. Rebecca will be working hard over the weekend to have them graded by Monday."

I've already decided that I'm going to approach him when class is over. I'll never get good sleep again if I don't.

The girls hounded me before class about my being distant this semester. I don't think they're buying my excuses anymore, but

I just can't admit my struggles to them. I know they will want to fix it, and I don't want to be a burden.

My whole life, I've always been the poor girl who grew up without a mom. Who brought burnt cookies to the school bake sale, who didn't wear makeup or dress the right way when my dad was too busy working to worry about such trivial things.

I made a vow to myself in high school that as soon as things were in my control, I would never be that girl again.

Luke dismisses us, and I look around the room to see everyone else quickly exiting. Evening classes make people antsy, and they want out as soon as possible. I pack my things slowly, hoping nobody notices how long it's taking me to put my laptop in my bag.

Once most students are out of the room or at least climbing the stairs of the auditorium, I grab my bag and start to head in his direction. He looks up at me, and his warm smile instantly settles my nerves.

Just as I'm about to speak, Rebecca makes quick work to join us.

"Oh, I'm sorry. Go ahead, sweetie," she says like I'm a child. "I'll wait."

I'm momentarily filled with rage before I realize I have to come up with something to say that won't give away our... relationship. I don't even know what to call what we have going on right now.

When I look back at Luke, his eyes are slightly wider, looking alarmed. He's waiting for me to cover this up.

It hurts, but I get it. I have no right to be territorial over him.

"Um, I just wanted to tell you I really enjoyed the lecture today. I'm learning a lot in this class."

"Thank you, Savannah. I'm so glad you're absorbing the material. It will be valuable to you in your career."

I feel deflated at how distant we are acting right now. He is shuffling through his papers nervously, not meeting my eyes.

"Well, I'll see you on Wednesday. Bye."

I turn around and begin to walk up the steps, feeling embarrassed and small.

"Aww, looks like someone has a little crush on her professor." I hear Rebecca laugh behind me.

My fists clench at my sides as I listen to her not so subtly mock me. She must know I can hear her.

Feeling even more shitty than I did before class, I rush home so I can put on my pajamas and sulk.

When I get back, I grab Bailey and take her outside while it's still light out. I feel more confident today with my new pepper spray, sharp unicorn head, decorative things that can be used as weapons, and something that creates a brutally loud alarm sound. I spent all yesterday wandering around the city, searching for things to put on my keychain to fight off an attacker.

My phone rings, and I see my dad's name come up on the screen.

"Hey, Dad," I answer cheerfully.

I know he's doing his best to balance his new life with the one we had together. Just because it was always just me and him doesn't mean that's how it should be forever. He deserves happiness, and if that means I have to miss him a little more than I used to, I'm okay with that.

I couldn't deal with it if I told him I wasn't able to make this financial situation work. I know he would freak out and take a second job to provide for everyone, but he's sacrificed enough for me throughout my life.

"Hi, sweet pea," he says. "How's your final semester going?"

I smile at the nickname. He always called me sweet pea growing up. When I asked him where he got it from, he said it was because the flower means gratitude, and he's grateful for me every day.

"It's alright. Honestly, it's kind of dragging on. I just want it to be over."

He chuckles and gives me one of his favorite dad lines. "Don't try to race through life, honey. It can become a habit."

My father always has words of wisdom for random situations. It's annoying at times, but it's weirdly helpful at others.

"Yeah, yeah, yeah. Hold the lecture. Good girl, Bailey," I praise her for her quick work of going potty, and then we both run back inside.

"So, how are Veronica and the kids?" I ask, wondering if it will ever not feel awkward knowing my father has an entire other life happening without me.

"They're great. Actually, I'm calling because Veronica was wondering if you were going to be home for spring break at all. She wants to have the house perfect. I told her she's being ridiculous and that you weren't going to walk around inspecting the dust on the mantel, but there's no talking sense into her," he jokes.

I laugh at the thought of my dad trying to talk sense into a woman when it comes to cleaning for a guest. I'm only twenty-two, and even I already know that particular conversation is a losing battle.

"That's really sweet that she's so worried about it. I'll probably be home on April 3rd and stay for a few days, but there is a slight chance I won't be back at all..." I trail off, unsure if I should have said anything in the first place. The odds are slim that I'll be so lucky to win, but I should still warn my dad and Veronica in case the universe is on my side.

"Oh? You thinking of going somewhere with friends?" he asks.

Ha! It's comical to think I am financially secure enough to jet off to a beach somewhere with my friends for a week... I wish!

"Actually... I *could* be in Italy."

"Italy? Why in the world would you be in Italy?" he asks.

"It's for school. One of my professors owns a wine distribution company. Whoever gets the highest grade on one of our assignments gets to go with him to one of his meetings with a potential client in Italy. It's all expenses paid, and it'd be a really beneficial hands-on experience for me."

Gosh, saying it out loud to someone as a real possibility and considering what it would entail has my entire body reacting with nervous energy. I would be spending a week in Italy *alone* with Luke. Despite having just made an ass of myself in front of him, the idea of us on an Italian getaway makes my heart race.

"Wow, what an amazing opportunity. I bet you'll win. I'll have to tell Veronica to count you out for spring break."

"Come on, Dad. There's over a hundred students in my class. The chance of me winning is extremely low."

I pour myself a glass of wine and sit on my small loveseat, covering myself with a fuzzy cream blanket. When my phone starts to buzz against my ear, I steal a glance and see that I got a text message from Luke.

"Dad, I'm getting a call. I gotta go," I say eagerly.

"I know, I know. It's your senior year. You don't want to be stuck on the phone all night with your father. I'll talk to you soon. Love you."

"Love you too, Dad."

I hang up and immediately open up my text messages.

Luke: I'm sorry we got interrupted tonight—again. That seems to happen to us a lot. We still need to finish that tiebreaker.

I can't help but smile at the thought that he's initiated contact this time, which I think—I *hope*—means that he's been thinking about me just as much as I've been thinking about him.

Me: I'm surprised you're willing to risk getting stomped on again. I'm feeling fast tonight.

Luke: Just meet me in the game, Princess.

That nickname... I thought maybe it was a one-time deal, but I love that he's still using it.

I open the game and find him waiting for me. It prompts us to click when we're ready to start, and then we're off. When I see the theme of the puzzle, I almost drop my phone. Kinky Word

Search. What the hell is this? Are we in some adult game that I'm not aware of?

I don't even have time to think about it because I need to win.

Okay, first word is...

"Oh, come on!" I shout.

Age Play.

I fly through the puzzle, ignoring the obvious prank the universe is playing on us right now, and feel more motivated than ever to kick his ass.

The words on this sheet are sure as hell kinky: Begging. Discipline. Roleplay. Voyeur. Flogging. Submission. Restraint. Power Exchange.

I find the final word and see *Winner!* dance across the screen. Victory feels meaningless at this point when all I can think about is what went through his mind when he picked this puzzle and saw the word choices.

I click on his call from the other night, not pausing to consider if I want to video chat or call him. His face comes up immediately, but I see no signs of amusement from his little prank.

"Did you think that would be funny, Savannah?" he asks in a warning tone.

"Me?" I gasp in surprise. "I had *nothing* to do with that. I thought that was you."

"Really?" His eyebrows raise in question, making him look annoyingly adorable. "You're telling me we somehow stumbled upon a very R-rated puzzle by chance?"

"It wasn't me!" I raise my voice. "You're the one who picked the options this time, I just met you in the game."

Upon closer inspection, I notice he isn't wearing a shirt, and there are white pillows and an expensive-looking wooden bed-frame behind him. His skin looks smooth and tan, even in the dead of winter.

"I just went in and clicked on the..." he stops abruptly. "Oh, shit."

"What? What happened?"

His eyes meet mine through the screen. "I may have clicked on the eighteen and older button when going through the options."

"Oh, really? So, it was you who made me look for things like Anal Training and Katoptronophilia? I don't even know what the hell that is," I joke.

There's no humor on his side of the line. I'm not actually trying to make him feel bad, I can tell it was an honest mistake.

"Mirrors," he says with quiet emphasis.

I stop and think for a second. What the hell is he talking about?

"Mirrors?" I question.

"Katoptronophilia. It's about getting off by having sex in front of mirrors, princess." His hoarse whisper makes me shiver.

It feels like all the air in the room has been sucked out, making it harder to breathe. His gaze looks me over seductively while he waits eagerly for my reply.

"Have you ever?" I find myself asking.

I should have laughed it off and made fun of him for knowing what it meant. It would be the smart way to veer this conversation into safer territory, but I don't seem to be very good at playing it safe where Luke is concerned.

"Have I ever what, princess?" he asks as he rests his head up on his hand. The bulge of muscles in his arm is prominent and extremely distracting. "Have I ever fucked in front of a mirror?"

I mimic his position while trying to contain the feelings his words evoke. I don't trust the words I want to speak to make it out of my mouth, so I just nod my head.

"No, actually, I never have. What about you?" he replies, his stare bold and assessing.

I shake my head back and forth.

A wicked smile spreads across his face. "Are you at a loss for words?" I nod again, seemingly the only response I can manage at the moment, and he laughs as if sincerely amused. "What I would do if I were with you right now..."

"What..." I start, but my voice breaks. I try again. "What would you do?"

His burning eyes have me waiting with bated breath.

"This is such dangerous territory right now, princess," he says, slightly shaking his head and looking away.

I'm so pent up from weeks of this energy crackling between us. I decide enough is enough, I need a release. Mustering all the courage I have, I wait until his eyes meet mine again and ask, "If we aren't technically touching each other, would it be so bad?"

I watch him bite his lip while he ponders my words. After what feels like an eternity, he smiles.

"I've been tortured here since we started talking, wondering what those tits look like underneath that small tank top. They've been peeking out of the top, teasing the fuck out of me. I want you to pull a strap down slowly until it exposes one of those beautiful breasts."

Holy. Shit.

I'm not sure I had even the slightest clue what I was asking for, but he is diving right in. This is clearly a man who has experience, nothing compared to what I've been exposed to. With one sentence, he's already made my body feel like it's never felt before. It's like there's this electric current running through me making every part feel more sensitive than ever before—like a single touch could set me off.

I don't want this to end, I never want it to end, so I do as he says.

I rest my phone against the blanket, still lying on my side, and bring my hand up to my shoulder. My thumb and pointer finger grab onto the strap and slowly bring it down a couple inches. He watches intently as I let it slide off my shoulder completely.

I move my hand to the top of my tank and pull it down, exposing my right breast to him. Fuck, it feels so amazing to let this man see me like this.

"Fuuuck, princess. Look at your perfectly pink nipple. It's erect and begging to be sucked on. Pinch it for me, and tell me how it feels," he demands.

I obey his command and a small moan escapes me. It feels like he's actually here doing this to me.

"It feels rough but perfect. I wish it were your hands on me," I cry. "I think about it all the time."

"More, beautiful. Show me more," he begs.

It's hot seeing him so worked up and knowing that I'm the reason for it.

"I need to see you," I say seductively as I continue to touch myself. "It's only fair, Professor Luke."

He gives me a stern look, and just when I think he's going to stop after I reminded him of his position over me, he puts his hand on his chest and starts to caress it down his bare chest. His camera follows as it runs across the most beautiful chest and set of abs I've ever seen.

"You're playing with fire, Savannah," he taunts.

My breath hitches. When he gets to the top of his gray sweatpants, he stops, leaving the camera on his stomach. I miss his face, but hell if I don't want to see what happens next.

"You get more when I get more, princess," he says, bringing my nickname back.

If anyone else tried to call me princess, I would throw a fit, but coming from him, it sounds endearing and sexy when used in this context.

"What do you want me to do?" I ask him.

"Touch yourself. Tell me if you're wet," he instructs.

I reposition my camera so my hips are in the shot, then slide my hand into my black sweatpants. My fingers slide straight into my entrance which is completely drenched.

"I'm soaked," I tell him, then bring my fingers up to my clit and start to rub.

The pressure is exactly what I need, working to curb the ache in me as I whimper in relief.

"I see your arm moving, rubbing yourself. Show me, princess. I want to see you give yourself this pleasure."

"You first," I request. "I want to see you touch yourself."

He grunts. "You want to see what you do to me? You have no idea, princess. My world has changed in the brief time since you've come into it. All I do is think of you. Whether I'm awake or asleep, my brain lives in a world filled with images of you."

I think I gasp at his words, but when he pulls his sweats down, I lose my breath entirely. He is huge, thick, and long. His hand grips his massive erection as he starts to run it slowly up and down. I think my jaw has hit the bed in shock as I watch the best thing to ever play across the screen of my phone.

My fingers work faster on myself, rubbing enthusiastically as I watch him.

"Fuck, Savannah. I wish this was your hand wrapped around my cock," he says. "Your turn, baby. Show me your pretty pussy."

I roll to my back and glide my pants down my legs.

I decide to move my phone down to an angle including my lady parts but so that the shot will still include my face at a distance. Apparently, I have some inner porn star in me that only Luke brings out.

I open my legs, revealing my bare pussy to him. Taking my pointer and middle finger, I separate my lips so he can see more of me.

"Fuck, princess. You really do have a perfect pussy. It's the sexiest thing I've ever seen." I look down at the screen and see that he is working himself with more vigor now. "Look at you glistening. Put your finger inside you, I need to see the way you suck it in."

I do as I'm told and moan as I start to hit my favorite spot.

"Dammit, you like that, don't you? You're gorgeous, Savannah. Inside and out. Keep going, play with yourself. Let me watch you make yourself come," he says.

We're both now playing with ourselves while our eyes are glued to the screen, watching what the other is doing. The room is a mix of moans, whimpers, dirty words, and demands.

"Ah, fuck. I'm gonna come all over myself," he announces.

I rub faster as I watch him moan through his release, thick ropes of cum spilling onto his stomach and fueling my own release.

"Ahh, Luke. Yes!" I hear myself scream as I continue with my movements until the feelings subside.

Silence falls upon the room, emphasizing the heaviness of our breathing. I move the camera back up to my face as I observe him while he looks at his ceiling. His stomach is still splattered in his cum, a sight that is never going to leave my brain.

He finally looks back over at his phone and breathes, "Wow."

"Yeah. Wow," I reply, my breaths coming to me a bit easier.

"I need to get cleaned up. I'll be right back," he says.

I nod my head and do the same, running to the bathroom and cleaning myself up. I grab a fresh pair of underwear and throw my sweatpants back on. When I get snuggled in bed, he's already there waiting for me.

He smiles. "You're so beautiful, Savannah."

I smile back. "Thank you."

"I wish you were here right now. I just want to be able to touch you."

I know that what just happened tonight is so far off limits, but that doesn't change the fact that nothing has ever felt so good... so right.

Chapter Ten

Luke

Idiot. That's what I am, a damn moron!

I've managed to make it through half of the semester without slipping up. How could I let that happen now? Is phone sex with a student really any better than the real deal? Even if it was the hottest thing I've ever done in my life, it was wrong.

And yet, afterward, I couldn't bring myself to make her feel bad about it. I wanted to be with her on the phone, even if only for a little while, pretend like we were two normal people who were allowed to spend time together.

I just need to make it through the next week and a half. As soon as it's spring break, I will be able to get some much-needed distance from Savannah.

Tonight will be the first time I've seen her since our phone call, and I'm debating on the best way to handle it. I don't want to completely avoid eye contact or act like she doesn't exist, but I need to remain strong. No googly eyes or smiles reserved just for her.

I'm a professional, and I need to start acting like it.

"What's crawled up your ass and died?" Marcus asks as we stand in front of the mirror, getting ready.

I work the tie through the loop, trying to focus on the task at hand. This has been the week from hell. Ignoring Savannah, even going so far as racing out of class before she can talk to me, has taken its toll, making me feel like a grade-A asshole.

"Will you stop asking me that?" I grumble. "I'm fine."

"Looking sharp, gentlemen." Gabe walks into the room wearing his tux.

He's a lucky bastard, marrying the woman of his dreams today. He's finally getting it all, and though I'm so relieved everything is finally working out for him, I'm also a jealous prick.

"He's talkin' about me." Marcus smiles to himself in the mirror.

"You're such a dumbass sometimes." I shove him as I walk by.

"You ready to get this party started?" Gabe smiles with excitement.

They landed on having the wedding at their house in Shaker Heights. They have a huge, enclosed tent in the backyard with heaters to keep the guests warm.

The ceremony goes smoothly, beginning with Alexis looking beautiful while her father walks her down the aisle. We are hustled to the large patio so they can break down the wedding ceremony seats and set up the dinner tables and dance floor.

I grab myself a glass of champagne from a waiter passing by and stand at one of the high-top tables, observing the guests and decorations.

"Everything turned out great, didn't it?" Pa asks as he settles in next to me.

I take another long swig of the champagne, which isn't landing hard enough for the kind of emotions swirling around inside.

"Yeah, I can't believe they put it together in less than two weeks."

Pa takes a sip of his wine. "You know your mother, just about anything can get done when she puts her mind to it."

I laugh at the accuracy of his statement. "Truer words have never been spoken," I say, struggling to add real enthusiasm to my tone.

"Something going on, son?" Pa asks.

"Why would you say that?"

He shrugs. "You just haven't been your usual easy-going self today. I thought I'd be pulling you off one of the many single younger ladies here tonight."

Are there single ladies here tonight? I hadn't even noticed. I guess that is unusual for me. I really am messed up over Savannah.

"It's nothing, Pa. Well," I begin to clarify, knowing that answer won't be enough for him, "nothing that I want to talk about at the moment."

He claps me on the back. "I'll give you a pass today since it's your brother's wedding. Next time, I won't let you off the hook so easily."

"Noted," I reply.

He walks away to mingle with the guests while I take another drag of the champagne, deciding this isn't going to cut it and that I need to switch to the hard stuff tonight.

My stomach growls when I see the hors d'oeuvres come out on silver platters, reminding me I skipped lunch today. I try to peer into the tent where the food is being prepared to get a hint what's for dinner, but when I do, I nearly drop my glass.

Savannah is here.

She's dressed in a black long-sleeve button-down shirt and black pants. She's carrying a tray of food and laughing at something another waiter just quipped from behind her. I didn't know she worked for a catering company, which is a stark reminder that I really know very little about her. I know what her breasts look like and the exact shade of pink her pussy turns when slicked in her arousal, but I didn't know she had a job.

My heart starts to race as I watch the waiter catch up with her and she gives him a carefree smile. He looks to be around her age, and one thing is clear: he fucking wants her.

I'm a man, I know when another man wants a woman.

She hasn't noticed me, and I'm not sure if I want her to or not. What good would come of it? I haven't been able to look at her without thinking of our phone call, and she deserves more than that.

"Let's go, bud." Marcus puts his arm around my neck. "They're ushering us back into the tent."

I follow his lead, noting Gabe and Alex have their own sweetheart table at the front of the tent, and take a seat at my family's table.

They've transformed the entire area to be lit up with candles, offering a romantic glow to the night.

"Excuse me, sir," someone says from behind me. "Can I top off your champagne?"

"No, thank you." I turn to the waitress. "I'm gonna grab a drink at the bar."

Just as I finish, I realize it's Savannah standing behind me.

An audible gasp leaves her lips, which catches the attention of Marcus and Pa. Leave it to these two men to notice a beautiful woman's actions even among the noise level of the room.

"Professor Luke," she says in shock.

"Savannah." I nod kindly, even though all I want to do is grab her and claim her as mine.

I see the way Marcus is looking her up and down right now. I give him the side eye, hoping he understands what it means.

Back. The. Fuck. Off.

"You're in Lucas's class?" Marcus leans against his chair, arm resting over the back. "You look much too old to be in college."

She smiles at him. "I graduate in two months."

Ahh. I guess that makes sense. So, tell me, is my brother just about the worst professor you've ever had?"

Her head bounces between the two of us, taking in the fact that she's speaking to my brother at the moment.

"Actually, he's an incredible professor. He's so passionate about the subject and brings so much real-world experience. I've learned a lot from him this semester."

I can feel her eyes on me, but I'm filled with so much guilt and embarrassment that I can't meet her gaze. I look past her with a tight smile and a firm nod of my head.

"Thank you, Savannah. It was nice to see you tonight."

Her face falls. I hate that I have to do this, but I need this moment to be over. I can't have my family finding out there is something going on between us, especially when I'm not sure how I'd even describe it.

"Nice to see you too, *Professor*," she replies in a sarcastic tone, then walks away.

Marcus whistles softly. "If that's what the college students are lookin' like these days, I think I may need to look into becoming a professor myself."

I punch his arm harder than I had originally intended.

"Ow, that hurt! What the fuck was that for?" He shoves me.

"Don't talk about my... student like that," I say, recovering from almost calling her my girl.

Shit, that could have been bad.

Pa gives me a curious look which makes me squirm in my seat, wondering what he's thinking. One thing I've learned is that you don't want to be on the receiving end of his disappointment. He has a way of making you feel horrible without saying much.

Servers begin serving dinner, waltzing in with large trays holding elegant plates of lobster, steak, short ribs, and salmon. The laughter surrounding me is only background noise to what my brain is focusing on. I spot Savannah walking in with that annoying ass guy on her tail again.

I lean back in my seat, scotch in hand, and follow her every movement. From the way she walks to the delicate slant of her neck to the loose hair falling from her ponytail. Everything about her is captivating.

She finds my eyes across the room and gives me a nasty scowl as she approaches my table. Her and the annoying punk set their trays on stands and begin to pass out the large family-style plates.

When she has to come to my side of the table and reach over my shoulder to put the plate in the last available spot in the center, I can't help but lean in toward her. She smells fresh with a nice floral scent to it, despite hauling ass on the job.

"I'm sorry," I whisper.

I hate her being mad at me, even if I was just trying to protect us. She could get in trouble too, and I would hate for this to ruin what she's worked so hard for.

Instead of responding, she just looks at me in a way that reveals her disappointment. Damn, did she learn that from Pa? She's good at it.

Once the plates are out, they pick up their things and start to walk back the way they came in. I watch the guy put his hand on her lower back, and that's all it takes. I'm up and out of my seat in an instant, excusing myself to use the restroom.

As they approach the side of the house, I see his hand reach for her again, and instinct takes over. "Princess," I shout.

She stops abruptly and turns around. "Excuse me?" she answers.

"You know this guy?" her friend questions. He looks back at me with disdain as he sizes me up.

"Go ahead," she tells him. "I'll be right there."

He gives me a once-over from head to toe before turning around and walking away. Savannah faces me, arms crossed, as she waits for my next move.

"Who is he?" I ask as I close the distance between us.

Her eyes follow me, analyzing my every move as I stop right in front of her, hands in my pockets.

"What?" she asks.

"That guy." I point in his direction. "Something going on between you two?"

When in the world have I ever been the jealous type? Never. This feeling is new for me, and I can't say that I'm a fan.

"Who, Declan?" she asks. "Are you serious? No, nothing's going on between the two of us."

My hands remain rigid in my pockets. "He wants you."

"No, he doesn't. We're just friends."

"Yes, he does. It's obvious."

Her arms fall to her sides as she rolls her eyes. "Whatever. If he does, I don't see how it would concern you, *Professor* Luke, seeing as you've ignored me all week. Not to mention dismissing me at your family's table like I am nothing more than the help to you. Like I'm nobody of significance."

She starts to walk away, but I gently grab her arm and pull us behind a large maple tree. I press her against the trunk while my hands rest on two branches above her head, caging her in. It wasn't my intention to get so close to her, but I can feel her breath on my lips.

"What are you doing, Luke?" she weakly asks.

"I'm sorry, Savannah."

She looks into my eyes, her face clouded with sadness.

"So, I'm not your princess anymore?"

My chin falls to my chest as my shoulders collapse. I grip the tree branches hard enough to feel them scratch my skin, but I welcome the pain. It's a brief distraction from the agony of knowing that I let her down.

"I'm just trying to protect both of us," I whisper. When I look up, I see the glistening of her eyes. "Princess..."

A bitter laugh escapes her, and then she shakes her head. "Don't do that. I love it when you call me that. Don't say it out of pity." A small tear slips down her cheek which she wipes away quickly, as if she's embarrassed. "Does that mean I'm up for grabs tonight? If Declan makes a move, I shouldn't stop him?" she suggests.

She's testing my strength, trying to see if I could really give her up that easily. As much as I want to be that man, the one to snap and tell her she's mine... I can't.

Chapter Eleven

Savannah

I hold my breath as I wait for his response. I don't know what we're doing. I know it's wrong, but I just can't help myself around him.

Seeing him tonight, among the glow of the lights, the way he fills out a suit... It's all just too much. Add that to the dejected feelings I've had all week as he did everything in his power to avoid eye contact with me during his lectures.

Then he has the nerve to be jealous when a coworker simply jokes around with me? I'm as mad at him as I am excited that he cares enough to be jealous.

"You're free to do what you want, Savannah," he says. He remains in place, towering over me with his long arms and bulging muscles, and I need him to go away.

Tears are threatening to spill over, and he is the last person I want to witness this, realizing how stupid it is to feel this way over a man I've never even touched. We barely know each other, and what happened the other night wasn't exactly a real interaction between the two of us, but every second of it felt like something special— something amazing.

"Can you please step away from me, Professor Luke?" I ask, making it clear that I see the line he's drawn in the sand.

He looks down at me with a pained expression before he pushes off the tree and moves to the side.

No other words are spoken. I walk away quickly, trying to find an area where I can have a mini meltdown. I come to a stop in between the servers' tent and a fence, and it's there, standing in the cold, dark night, where I let my feelings take over.

My shoulders shake as tears run down my cheeks.

How could I be so stupid to think that he would just continue down this path? He's my *professor*. He doesn't want anything to happen that would tarnish his reputation.

Okay, no more tears tonight. You had your little moment of self-pity, Savannah. Time to be the adult that you are and get back to work.

When I walk back, I see my coworkers huddled in a corner, shoving their faces with food. I take a plate off the table and load up some dinner for myself and then join them.

"You good, Davis?" Declan asks from his spot on top of the cooler.

I put on a brave face, smiling my brightest smile. "I'm good. Starving."

When I take a seat next to Jill, I realize this is where I belong: eating scraps from the rich people's leftovers. I'm a world away from Luke and his fancy life in the main tent.

Despite all the running around I've done and how much my body wants the food, I'm finding my appetite is ruined. I pick around the plate, hoping nobody notices how much I've left uneaten.

"Dessert time, everybody," Kylie, our manager, calls. "Clean yourselves up. I don't want anyone looking sloppy out there."

We all get rid of our plates and inspect our uniforms to make sure everything's in place.

"How do you know him?" Declan comes up beside me, straightening his tie.

"It doesn't matter," I reply. "Let's just get this night over with."

He puts his arm around my neck.

"I'm no idiot, *princess*." He uses my nickname jokingly. "Let's make this man's night a shitty one."

I glance over at him and see his mischievous grin. "What are you talking about, Dec?"

"For the rest of the night, you're my girl," he says with a wink.

Damn. I kind of like the sound of that. What's the worst that could happen if I make Luke a little jealous? It's my right as a woman to show a man what he's missing out on, even if he is trying to be honorable.

I walk over to the dessert display as the staff is plating the food on white and gold—probably real freakin' gold—china.

Declan comes over with our trays. We fill them up with cheesecake, crème brûlée, macarons, tiramisu, and more. My stomach growls in appreciation for the sugary treat aroma that drifts through the air. No matter the state of my nerves, I've never backed down from desserts. I suppose that's how I know I'll be okay, as long as my body isn't betraying me by refusing sugar.

I already know I'm going to town on these desserts by the end of the night. Rich women never eat much, so I'm sure there will be a lot leftover.

Declan helps me put the tray on my shoulder and leads the way to the main tent with our stands on his other shoulder. He's been a great partner in this gig, always helping out with the heavy lifting of the job.

Clearly, he's a good friend as well, since he's willing to play along with the drama in my life.

We walk through the clear plastic walls of the tent, working to keep the heat in. I do my best to not even glance in the direction of Luke.

After our trays are safely placed on the stands, Declan and I begin putting the options down in the center of the table. With every move I make, Declan whispers something in my ear to make me laugh.

It's all gibberish, he's just trying to get me to react.

When we're in front of Luke, I lean down and put a piece of tiramisu in front of him. Declan leans over me to do the same as his hand lands on my lower back then slides to my ass as we stand up straight.

Luke grumbles and says something under his breath, and his brother witnesses the entire thing with a huge smile on his face.

"Did you guys know this beautiful young lady here is a student of Luke's?" his brother announces to the rest of the table.

Their father chokes on his drink as a chuckle escapes him. Declan looks over at me with wide eyes, not realizing the man we're making jealous is my professor. He recovers quickly, winks at me, and gets right back to work.

Great, now he thinks I'm a whore. I'm so happy my life can be the source of entertainment for so many people tonight.

The lady sitting next to Luke's father, presumably his mother, speaks. "Oh, how lovely. We're so proud of Lukie for taking that on with everything else he has going on."

Lukie?

I think it's sweet that his mother calls him that, but when I look down at him, his hand is on his forehead as he shakes his head.

"We are so proud of you, *Lukie*." His brother pats his back.

"He's a great professor," I say with affection.

I'm still furious with him, but that doesn't mean I like seeing him embarrassed or being picked on by his family, even if I know it's all in good fun.

Instead of standing around to hear the rest of the conversation play out, I follow Declan away with our empty trays. When we get to the back of the space, he puts his arm around me and squeezes my side, then leans in to whisper in my ear. "You didn't tell me he was your professor."

When we pull away, he's looking back toward Luke's table, but he somehow manages to wink at me.

Once we're out of the tent, I break free from his hold. "Shit, you really know how to play this game."

"It comes naturally," he says with a shrug. "Now let's get back to the fact that you're not the innocent girl I thought." He throws his arm around my neck jokingly. "Are you *sleeping* with your professor?"

"What? No! I'm not, I swear."

He laughs loudly. I know it doesn't seem like I'm telling the truth given the circumstances, and I can tell he doesn't believe me. Before we can enter the tent, a strong hand wraps around my wrist, gently yanking me back.

"Not so fast, princess," the familiar voice snaps.

"What do you want, Professor?"

Instead of answering, he pulls me away and starts to lead me to the opposite side of the house. It's vacant and dark on this side, leaving us alone.

"What are you doing?" I snap. "I'm gonna get fired if I go missing."

He flips me around and invades my space until I'm pushed up against the house. The cold stone makes me shiver—or maybe it's the handsome man standing in front of me whose radiating anger is seriously affecting my body.

"No, you're not. I'm sure we're paying this catering company enough money to tell them we can steal their staff away if we choose to." He moves closer to me. "Now, tell me. Are you trying to drive me crazy with your little *friend,* or is there really something going on between you two?"

Ugh, he seriously has some nerve playing me like a pinball. I push his chest in an effort to give myself some much-needed space, but he doesn't budge.

"I don't need to answer you. You were the one who said it not even an hour ago: I'm free to do what I want."

I barely get the words out before his lips come crashing down on mine. They're aggressive and demanding. His hands are on my face, fingers reaching behind my neck while his thumbs caress my cheeks.

"Fuck, princess. I'm so crazy over you," he whispers into my mouth.

This kiss is more than anything I've ever experienced. His tongue slowly traces my lips, making my body shiver in response as a soft moan escapes me. When his lips capture mine again, our tongues meet with hunger and urgency. I try to keep up but succumb to the forceful domination of his lips as he takes control.

Just as I finally relent, cold air hits me as he lets go and steps away.

"Shit, I shouldn't have done that." He begins to pace back and forth while his hand rubs the back of his neck.

My lips burn in the aftermath of his fiery kiss. I'm too wrapped up in what just happened to really register what he's saying.

"I gotta go," he mutters as he starts to back away. "I'm sorry."

I fall back against the house, my breathing still ragged, wondering how the hell I'm ever going to recover from a kiss like that.

I shake my head, knowing I don't have the time to deal with this right now. I have to get back to work and hope like hell nobody noticed my absence. I can't afford to lose this job when I'm already barely making ends meet.

I thought I was indecisive, my father always telling me to pick a shoe and move on with my life, but Luke's inability to figure out what he wants puts my shopping dilemmas to shame.

Chapter Twelve

Savannah

"Hey, girl," Tricia says as she takes a seat next to me and wraps me in a hug. "Thanks for coming out with us Saturday night. We've missed you. It was nice to have the whole gang back together."

In spite of my foul mood, I laugh at her dramatics.

"I've missed you guys, too. Saturday was so fun, and I hate that I've had to bail on so many nights out. I've just been trying to pick up extra shifts whenever I can."

She looks at me skeptically, like she knows there's more I'm not saying. I hate that I feel the need to hide my struggles from her, but I'm not ready to tell my friends how dire my situation is.

Aubrey and Shannon slide in the seats behind us and Shannon immediately leans down between Tricia and me and says, "You guys ready to see me win the trip to Italy? Sexy Italian men, here I come!"

All the girls are giggling at that, so I join in, even though I'm not finding any humor in hearing who wins the trip. As much as I want to go, I don't know if I could even enjoy it with the way things are going between Luke and me. Spending an entire week with him while on a roller coaster of emotions sounds exhausting. At this point, the only thing making me desperate to go is the idea of getting a week away from my shithole apartment.

Every time I have to take Bailey outside, I recall the look in those two guys' eyes, and it's enough to keep me up at night in fear.

Professor Luke stands at the front of the hall with a smile on his face. "Well, class! Today's the day. Who here is ready to find out who got the best grade and gets to come to Italy with me?"

The whole class erupts in cheers and applause—well, everybody but me as I sink further into my seat.

"I had Rebecca put the winner's name in an envelope. It will be news to me as well. I went through and checked all of her grading but never tallied the percentages to see who came out on top."

Rebecca sits in the corner of the room, smugly waving at us, acting like her and Luke are in on something we aren't. I can't stand her.

"We are going to wait until the end of class to make the announcement," Luke announces, making everybody groan. "I know, I'm anxious for the results too, but it will be hard to pay attention after the announcement."

You would think the ninety-minute class would go by as slow as molasses waiting in anticipation, but I've been so lost in my own head thinking about Friday night that I'm startled when I realize there's only five minutes left.

Luke takes off his glasses—yes, glasses are apparently a new addition to his sexy professor look. He claims his contacts were bothering him, so he needed to switch it up today.

How many other girls in this class are having tiny orgasms watching him down there? Am I the only one messed up in the head?

Although, none of them know what his lips feel like against theirs. They don't know how powerful his kisses are, how they leave your world turned upside down wondering what just happened. Only I do. I know what it feels like when his tongue presses against yours while his hands hold your head in place so he can take what he wants.

His eyes land on mine for the first time today and my heart starts to beat erratically in my chest. I think I see a quick change in his eyes, a flicker of emotion, but it's gone.

"I think it's time we find out which one of you are going to Italy with me." He turns off the screen as the class once again gets pumped up.

I sit back in my seat and chew the top of my pen anxiously. I don't actually think I'm going to win, but it's still nerve-racking.

"Rebecca," he says as he holds out his hand for the envelope.

She stands up from the corner of the room, sticking her chest out way too eagerly for everyone to see. Is she just an attention whore, taking it wherever she can get it?

"Okay, class." He looks around the room with a smile, not making eye contact with me. "The winner of the Italy trip, who gets to experience first-hand what it's like to make a deal internationally, is..."

The envelope gets torn open, and then he pulls out a piece of paper folded in half. My hand grips my pen so hard I can feel my nails start to dig into my skin. *Don't be a pretty girl, please don't be a pretty girl.*

I won't be able to handle knowing he's going to spend an entire week alone with some other young college girl.

He opens the piece of paper and looks down. The grin on his face disappears for a moment as he blinks down at it, but he catches his hesitation and plasters the smile back on.

"Savannah Davis," he says then looks over at me. "Congratulations, you've received the highest grade on the paper and therefore will be accompanying me to Italy next week."

My girls are hooting and hollering around me.

"Shit, girl." Shannon pushes my shoulder. "I'm so damn jealous of you right now."

I smile the brightest smile I can muster, but even I know it's a weak attempt. How can I be excited when he looks horrified?

"My assistant will be in touch with you to iron out the details, Savannah."

I nod my head as my fingers still grip tightly to my pen. When I look over at Rebecca, she's staring daggers at me. Does she recognize me as the girl she called out for having a *cute crush on the professor*? Now I'm going to be alone with him in Italy for a week, and she clearly isn't happy about that.

I could be projecting all of this onto her. For all I know, she's a sweet person and really did think my behavior in front of Luke was cute. Maybe she has resting bitch face and isn't actually glaring at me right now.

Well, resting bitch face or not, it's making me uncomfortable.

"Well, that concludes everything we needed to cover for tonight. We'll pick back up again on Wednesday."

"You're going to freakin' Italy." Aubrey shakes me with excitement. "Why the hell aren't you more excited?"

"I think I'm just in shock," I lie.

"This calls for a celebration. Come on, let's go to Mac's for some drinks," Tricia says.

"Totally! We need to celebrate the fact that this time next week, our girl is going to be flirting her ass off with some sexy Italian with an accent," Shannon says.

"I actually need to get back to Bailey. She hasn't been feeling well," I lie again, immediately noticing the disappointment in their eyes. I've started to resent this part of me that can't just say what's actually going on in my life. I don't know when I became someone who had to keep so many truths from my friends.

"I hope Bailey feels better," Aubrey says as they start to file out. "We'll see you around."

As much as I want to see Luke right now to talk about what happened on Friday, I have no interest in Rebecca making me feel like a child again. I grab my things then shuffle up the stairs and out the door.

The weather is finally starting to turn from winter to spring. My jeans and sweater are enough today, no winter coat or gloves needed.

I take my time walking to my car, enjoying the fact that it's not blistering cold. As I make my way, it hits me that I'm going to Italy. *Italy*. Holy shit. Despite the shock on Luke's face when reading my name, I smile.

It's a dream come true knowing that I'm going to be in Tuscany this time next week. So me and Luke had a little slip up and kissed... It's not the end of the world. I've realized I may have been unfair to him, thinking that just because we got carried away on our video call, he owed me something.

He's my professor, after all. Everything about us together is wrong. And who knows, maybe after the semester's over, we can revisit the possibility of *us*.

Funny what a trip to Italy can do to one's perspective. Turns out, I just needed something to look forward to, to pull me out of this funk I've been in.

I open the door to my car to get in, shuffling my bag off my shoulder.

"Savannah," Luke's deep voice calls from behind me.

I turn around and see him jogging my way. Ugh, this all would be so much easier if he weren't so good-looking.

"Savannah." He breathes heavily when he reaches me. "I'm sorry."

"Luke—" I try to speak, but he keeps going.

"I'm so sorry. I know I'm failing you miserably. I'm clearly such a fuck up at this professor thing. I just wanted you to know that none of this is your fault and—"

I cut him off. "*Luke*. Stop it. You don't need to apologize. I'm just as guilty as you. None of this should have happened. It's wrong. From now on, let's just forget about it." I shrug my shoulders. "Maybe we can revisit the idea after the semester if we're both still interested."

He seems caught off-guard. "You would wait?" he asks, looking both hopeful and skeptical.

"I think you might be worth it," I tell him with a smile.

Amusement flickers in his eyes. "I'd say the odds are in your favor. If our kiss was anything to go off, a lifetime of waiting would be worth it for me."

I look to the side, needing to break the emotions his words have evoked. "Let's try to cool it on saying things like that right now. This is already hard enough."

He bites his lip with satisfaction then takes a step toward me.

"So, Italy, huh? Congratulations, Miss Davis."

"Thank you." I give him a bright, wide smile.

He shakes his head. "A toothy grin like that makes all of this worth it. I'm so happy you're going to get this experience."

"I'm so excited."

"I have to say, I was shocked to see your name. What are the odds? An auditorium full of students, and you're the winner."

I cross my arms across my chest. "Are you saying you don't think I'm smart enough to have actually gotten the highest score?"

He throws his head back and lets out a big peal of laughter. "Savannah, I know how smart you are, but each student had a .6 percent chance of winning. I wasn't going to hold my breath hoping it was you."

"But you wanted it to be me?"

"With everything in me, I wanted it to be you."

I take in a shaky breath. "Okay, I need to get away from you right now. When I see you on Monday for Italy, please try to be a bit more of a dick."

He tucks a piece of hair behind my ear. "I'll do my best, princess."

With both hands on my hips, I give him my best annoyed look at his inability to follow a simple request.

"You asked me to be a dick starting Monday," he says as he backs away with a wink. "I'll see you in class on Wednesday... *Savannah*."

"Bye, *Professor* Luke," I bite back.

He shakes his head but doesn't lose the hint of amusement in his eyes.

When I get into my car, I have to let out a girly scream of excitement. I'm going to Italy with a man I'm pretty sure I'm falling for, despite my best efforts. And we both agreed we can wait until the semester is over.

What could go wrong?

Chapter Thirteen

Luke

"Everything squared away with the university? Are you meeting the student at the airport?" Marcus asks while Vino is cuddled up on his lap.

My dog does this every time my suitcase is out and packed. She gets sad and distant, seeming angry that I'm daring to leave her again. I hate being apart from her for even a week, but at least I know I'll be on the receiving end of her endless affection when I get back.

"Yeah, we're meeting at the security check."

"Alright. Good luck, bro. Show Mr. Mancini what it'd be like to work with us."

Marcus winks at me, then snuggles into Vino, knowing that it'll annoy me.

I grab my suitcase and walk out, but not before giving him the finger. His laugh echoes behind me as I close the door.

I've parked my car in the long-term parking lot and am in line for airport security, all within forty minutes. I used to take a car service each time I had to fly, but I found that after a long trip back home, I like getting into my own car and not having to deal with anyone else.

I'm standing in the airport security area when I get a phone call from a carrier company for one of our suppliers. I've been hounding them for days trying to straighten out a delay of a large order that we put in weeks ago.

"Luke Giannelli," I answer.

"Hello, Mr. Giannelli. This is Marshall at Carrier For You. I received word that you've been trying to get ahold of me."

"Yes, I have been for a while now. I trust you've been brought up to speed on the matter," I say as I pace back and forth.

"I see one of your orders was delayed in Rome. We're so sorry for any inconvenience. We had an emergency order come through that took priority. I assure you that your order is on a plane and will make it to your warehouse tomorrow."

Unbelievable. This little prick just admitted that he grounded my order for someone else to receive theirs sooner.

"Well, I don't feel assured. When I agree to and pay for a specific delivery date, I expect you to honor your end of the deal. I have some very important clients who are waiting for their order, and telling them someone else's order was more important is not an option."

"I understand why you're upset bu—" he starts, but I cut him off.

"No, I don't think you do. If you did, you would—" I begin, but the words get stuck in my throat.

Savannah is standing in front of me in tight yoga pants and a cashmere cream sweater. Her hair is down in loose waves, and her makeup is minimal. She looks... stunning.

Her sweet smile makes me feel things.

"Mr. Giannelli. I'm sorry, did I lose you?" Marshall talks through the phone, getting my attention.

"No, I'm here. Just don't let it happen again," I say to him while my eyes hold Savannah's. I hang up the phone and smile.

"Sounds like somebody's in trouble," she jokes. "No need to stop on my account."

"I'm not interested in talking to that person for a second longer when you're in front of me." My eyes drift back down her body. "You look beautiful."

She looks down at herself. "I was trying to look presentable but comfortable. A ten-hour plane ride while stuck in those tight seats calls for comfy clothes."

"Ah, I get it. I guess I'm gonna be a bit uncomfortable then," I say.

She looks at my jeans and gray button-down shirt. "It's not what I would have picked for a long flight, but you look good."

"Come on, let's get through this line."

We both put our luggage on the conveyor belt and walk through the metal detector, bypassing security without issue. I hate having to take off my shoes in public, though. It makes me feel defenseless being shoeless in front of so many strangers. I pause and wonder if I'm the only weird one who feels this way or if we're all thinking the same thing as we obey the rules like it's normal. At least it's winter, and we're all in socks.

Savannah starts to walk toward the main terminals, but I stop her and grab her hand.

"It's this way," I instruct.

She follows me, confusion evident in her every move. I may have left out some details about the travel.

I lead her onto an elevator to the airport shuttle, which takes us to a completely different part of the airport.

"Where are we going?" she asks as we step off.

We walk into a waiting area that is surrounded by glass which gives us a perfect view of several small planes out on the tarmac.

"We're going to Italy," I say with a smile.

She gives me a stern look. "Luke, seriously."

I grab her hand and pull her along behind me.

"Hi, we're here for our flight," I say to the lady behind the desk as I hand her our information. "Ah, Mr. Giannelli. Your plane is ready. Just go ahead and take a seat, and your pilot will be with you soon."

"Thank you."

I lead Savannah to the seats.

"Between me and my siblings, one of us is always traveling for work. Most of the time, it's within the states. But when it's a longer trip like this, we rent a private jet."

She leans in like she didn't hear me. "Are you telling me I'm taking a *private jet* to Italy?"

My mouth twitches in amusement. "Yes, that's exactly what I'm telling you." She shoves my arm, and I feign injury. "What the hell? That's not the reaction I was expecting."

"Why didn't you tell me? I'm not dressed for a private jet. Everyone's going to think I don't belong."

"Who cares what you wear? There's not a damn thing you could put on your body that wouldn't make you the most beautiful woman in the room."

She opens her mouth to speak, but the words seem to get stuck. I raise my eyebrow, waiting for her to say something.

"Mr. Giannelli, my name is Louis. I'll be your pilot for the day."

I stand and shake his hand.

"Maria and Rylee here will get your luggage for you. Please follow us to your aircraft, where my co-pilot, Dean, is waiting. Don't hesitate to ask any questions you'd like. We're here for anything you need."

The stewardesses take our suitcases and lead us onto the tarmac. The gusts of the chilly April wind are more intense as we walk along the path. I turn around and see Savannah walking against the wind with her face hidden underneath the neck of her coat. I place my hand on her lower back, trying to make sure she gets to our aircraft safely.

Once we're aboard, Maria shows us around. There are six large cream seats with two large couches in the back. A bottle of champagne is chilling on ice in between two of the seats.

"Enjoy your flight," Maria says before moving to the front of the plane.

"You ready?" I ask Savannah as we buckle up.

She smiles, looking blissfully happy across from me. "I'm so ready."

The plane takes off, and we both sit silently in our seats as we look out the window. Once the seat belt light goes off, I unbuckle and reach for the bottle of champagne.

"You care for some celebratory bubbly?"

"I would love some," she replies as she sits up straight in her seat.

I pour the yellow-tinted contents into two glasses, handing one over to her, and then raise my glass.

"To a successful business trip, and hopefully some memorable experiences along the way."

My mouth curves into an unconscious smile as I stare at her infectious one. Our glasses clink together, and just like that, a trip I'll never forget is set in motion.

"Mmmm..." she moans. "This is *really* good."

I shift in my seat, my dick coming to life at her sounds. I get an image of her and me drinking wine this entire trip, the tastings we're going to be doing, and I know I'm in trouble.

We share a couple glasses together before I look down at my watch.

"Did you go to bed late last night?" I ask.

She nods. "Yep. I only got three hours like you told me."

"Good. It's near nine in Tuscany right now. Let's try to get some sleep so we're ready to go when we land."

I stand up and move to the back of the plane. The two couches are both large and extremely comfortable, so I've never had a problem getting decent sleep on them. I open the drawers beneath them and pull out blankets and pillows.

"Here." I hand her a sleep mask. "It'll block that light out and help you get to sleep sooner."

"Thanks," she says, taking it from my hand.

We both put them on top of our heads while we get ourselves comfortable on the couches. When I move to my side, she's in the same position, watching me intently.

"Hey, Luke," she whispers.

"Yeah?"

"Thank you for all of this. It's already the best trip of my life."

My heart beats rapidly in my chest.

"You're welcome, princess."

I pull my mask down and do my best to nod off, but it doesn't happen without a few dirty thoughts of the woman lying next to me.

Chapter Fourteen

Savannah

A dinging noise wakes me from my sleep. My bed feels different than I remember as I move around, trying to get comfortable. The noise sounds again, and I sit up. Am I wearing a sleep mask? What the hell—then it clicks. I'm on the plane. Correction: I'm on Luke's private jet.

I can't believe his company has this kind of money. I could tell by how he dressed and what he wore that he was wealthy, but I never imagined it was this level of wealth.

I pull my mask away and look over, expecting to see Luke's sleeping form, but instead, I only find an empty couch. No pillow or blanket in sight on his side.

A throat clears, and I glance around until I see him sitting in the chair we took off in. He's leaning back with his long, thick legs spread apart, wearing a devastating grin.

"Morning," he says as his face rests on his hand. "Welcome to Italy, princess."

"We're here?" I get up and join him.

"Should be starting our descent soon. They're just preparing our breakfast now."

Maria and Rylee come out moments later holding a large tray of food that I can already smell from here.

They turn the small table between Luke and me into a full one, then proceed to lay out food and coffee for us. There's fresh fruit and pastries that look to die for. My eyes survey the selections in front of me, not sure what to choose.

"I'd go for the Amalfi lemon cornetto. It's made with fresh lemons from the Amalfi coast. Cornettos are just Italian's play on a French croissant. In Italy, they make them slightly differently and fill them with different flavors. You'll get used to eating these as your breakfast with an Americano or espresso if you want to fit in with the natives."

As if on cue, my stomach rumbles at that. Even his description of the treat is like a food orgasm. I reach for the lemon cornetto and put it on my plate. Luke grabs the coffee carafe and holds it up.

"Coffee?" he asks.

"Please," I say, and he pours me a cup. "You know I can't resist a cup of coffee."

I bite into the lemon pastry, and *damn,* is it good! A little of the lemon curd gets stuck on my lip, so I lick it off, not wanting to waste a single drop. I close my eyes and enjoy the tang of the lemon and the sweetness of the dough. When I open them back up, Luke's eyes are sharp and assessing. I can't quite figure out what he's thinking, but there seems to be a hint of anger around him.

He grumbles something under his breath, but I'm too consumed by my food to care. I'm in Italy—well, flying into Italy—and eating amazing food already. I don't think there's much that can get me down.

The food and drinks are all cleared, and the table is put away as the plane starts to descend. I'm sitting excitedly in my seat as I look out the window. The ground gets closer and closer to us, inching me toward paradise. My hands are folded in my lap, and excited energy wants to burst out of me.

I'm trying to play it somewhat cool in front of Luke. This is just another day, another business trip for him, but for me... It's the trip of a lifetime.

The wheels hit the cement and bounce on and off the runway until we stay grounded and quickly come to a slow speed. The plane is parked, and Luke is leading me to the open door in no time. We walk down the stairs onto to the tarmac and are led to customs. As soon as we get to the other side of the building, a car is waiting for us, already packed with our luggage.

We get in and start the drive to Montepulciano, a medieval hilltop town only miles from the vineyard where we're staying. Apparently, this is the winemaker we are trying to convince to do business with Giannelli Family Selections.

Luke's assistant Maggie sent over the details a couple days ago. I've been doing research on the town, the wine in the area, and the family, trying to be as prepared as possible for the business side of the trip.

The wine made in Montepulciano is called Vino Nobile di Montepulciano, and I can't wait to try it.

As soon as we leave the airport, we're instantly driving through rolling hills with the classic Tuscan trees I've only seen in the movies. I feel like a little kid, my face almost pressed against the window glass. It's exactly as I pictured it, except even more beautiful in person.

The houses are all unique and yet exactly the same.

We slow down as we navigate gravel roads for what feels like miles. I'm too distracted by the beauty that surrounds me to pay attention. It's not until we come to a complete stop that I realize that we're here.

I turn to Luke, who already seems to have his eyes on me with a faint glint of humor.

"We're here," he says.

The driver comes to my side and opens the door for me, extending his hand to help me out. I take his hand willingly, enjoying the chivalry.

"Thank you," I tell him once I'm out.

I look up and see a large, beautiful villa in front of me made entirely of stone. To the right is a similar-looking villa but much smaller. Surrounding both buildings are so many grape vines that extend for miles, all on hills that appear to go on forever. In the distance, you can see a small town, which must be Montepulciano.

My breath is literally stolen away from me. It's all just so incredible.

Luke joins my side and looks out at the view.

"Breathtaking, isn't it?" he says.

"It's... There aren't even words."

His hand takes mine and leads me toward the large villa. An older gentleman walks out with a younger man following closely behind him. They have warm smiles on their faces and are wearing casual clothing, light sweaters and khakis.

When they reach us, the older man extends his hand to Luke, who drops my hand to shake his. I feel the loss immediately.

"Ciao. Benvenuto, Signor Giannelli," he greets warmly.

I don't know what it is about this place, about these people, but I feel instantly at home.

"Ciao. Grazie per averci," Luke responds.

Hold up... Are we only speaking Italian on this trip? I don't know Italian. Should I have been learning Italian all semester just in case I won? I studied up on it a little bit last week, but I only memorized select greetings and words.

I know ciao means hello and grazie is thank you, but everything else that's been said is fuzzy. I start to have an internal meltdown at the thought that I'm not going to understand a word that's said during this trip.

"E chi è questa bellezza?" the older man says while looking at me.

I glance nervously at Luke who just winks at me. That does nothing to calm my nerves.

"Lei non sa molto Italiano," Luke says as his head nods toward me.

Great, now they're going to talk about me in another language right in front of me, so I have no idea if they're saying good or bad things.

"Ah. Perdonami. Forgive me," he says to me as he takes my hand. "I speak English. Welcome to Mancini Farms. We're so happy to have you."

Oh, thank God! I may have overreacted a smidge just now. There's no way this trip would be all in Italian without a warning or heads up from Luke.

Mr. Mancini's thick Italian accent is exactly how I had imagined it to sound.

"Thank you so much for having me," I tell him. "I'm so looking forward to our stay."

"This is my son, Giovanni. Please let either of us know if you require anything to make your stay more comfortable."

His son steps forward and grabs my hand then leans in and kisses both cheeks. I'm not going to lie, his son is fine as hell.

"Ciao, bella," he says to me.

Okay, I know that means *hello, beautiful.* If an American said that to me upon meeting for the first time, I'd think he was a creep. But coming out of Giovanni's mouth, it just sounds downright sexy.

I turn to smile over at Luke, but instead, I notice his brows drawn together in an angry frown. I'm not sure what that's all about, but I turn back to Giovanni.

"Ciao. Thank you for having me."

"We take your bags," Mr. Mancini says as he and Giovanni grab our luggage from us. "Come, we show you your rooms."

The front door of the villa is made entirely of dark wood while the front porch is covered in pots filled with colorful flowers. When he opens the door, it's like we step into the past. The large room is mostly made of old stone and travertine tiles. The exposed wood columns on the ceiling are still in good condition but obviously date back to the origins of the villa.

There is a large brick fireplace in the back of the large room with a crackling fire giving off a warm and cozy ambiance. Chandeliers hang from the huge cathedral ceilings. The furniture looks relatively new but still in keeping with the era of the villa. It's all wood-framed, with cloths of different colors and textures covering the surfaces.

"Wow! Signor Mancini, this place is just incredible. Bellissimo," I say, attempting some of the Italian words I memorized.

"Ah. Grazie, signorina. Just this way," he says as him and Giovanni lead us up the tiled stairs.

I take in the pictures that cover the walls. Most are in black and white, clearly dating far back. Tons of them look like they were taken right here on the farm, picking grapes and smiling bright into the camera.

We get to the third floor, and they stop. There's a door to the left and one to the right.

"Signorina, you will be here. Signor just across the hall. We will let you two get settled for a bit, then we can take a tour of the grounds," Giovanni says as he and his father turn to head back down the stairs.

"Luke and Savannah will do," Luke says. "No need for all this formality."

Giovanni smiles. "Luke and Savannah. Please call us Giovanni and Giorgio."

"Why don't you go ahead and freshen up. I'll meet you by the fireplace in an hour?" Luke says to me once they're gone. "I'm going to take a quick shower."

I nod my head, agreeing that a shower sounds amazing right now. "Me too. I'll see you down there."

The room is huge. The same tiled floor remains throughout, while the wallpaper is a mixture of cream and tan colors. The dark wood beams are exposed in here as well. The king-sized bed looks plush and comfortable with a white down comforter. I walk over to the old wooden windows and push them open, immediately gasping at the view.

The Tuscan hills go on for miles, and they're right outside my window. Montepulciano is in view from here, and I make a note to ask Luke if we can explore. I walk over to a near dark curtain and pull it back, revealing a door leading out to a terrace. Baskets of flowers hang off the railing, with a small wrought-iron table and two chairs sit there waiting for me to have coffee while enjoying the view.

Magic. That's what it feels like.

I don't want to waste any time. I practically run to my suitcase and pull everything out. I'm not going to get my hair wet in the shower—something only woman with long, thick hair could possibly understand. Drying and styling my hair alone is a forty-minute process. I don't have time for that shit right now. I have a freakin' Tuscan farm to tour.

Chapter Fifteen

Luke

On my way down the stairs, I check myself in the old mirror hanging on the wall, blowing out a breath as I try to get ahold of myself. I keep reminding myself that there's no need to be nervous, this is just another business trip. I'm going to tour the farm with my future client and my student.

My white button-down shirt and khaki pants blend in with the feel of the vineyard. I'm wearing my expensive brown leather watch, giving the look a bit more sophistication. The cologne that I sprayed was purely habit, it has nothing to do with the woman I'm here with.

Keep telling yourself that, you idiot.

Ugh, I really hate my inner critic sometimes. Shut the fuck up.

When the fireplace comes into view, I lose my breath. The woman standing there in the white floor-length sundress with a small camisole on over it looks like a dream. Her hair is still down in loose curls.

My heart does something weird in my chest.

She turns around and smiles when she sees me. I try to play it cool as I walk toward her even though my hands are itching to reach for her.

"Wow." Her eyes look me up and down. "You clean up pretty nice, Professor Luke."

I hate the reminder that I'm her professor when she doesn't feel like my student, especially not here, but I know that's partly why she's calling me that. I force a small smile.

"Are you okay?" she asks, looking at me knowingly.

"I'm good. I think I'm just getting a little mixed up from travel."

"Aww. Is the old man feeling jet-lagged?"

I'm not fucking old. I want to grab her hand and drag her upstairs to show her just how young I am. I bet no fucking punk frat-boy has ever made her feel half as good as I can.

"I'm sure I'll be fine," I say to deflect what her comment did to me. "You look beautiful, princess."

Her eyes sparkle. I know she likes my nickname for her, and right now it's my way of countering her "professor" comment and reminding her of what we could be.

"Ah, Luke, Savannah." Giorgio comes out of a door in the back. "You two look lovely. Are you ready for the tour?"

"Looking forward to it, Giorgio," I say.

While doing business in Italy, I've learned that first and foremost, you let them be the host in the beginning. This is their life's work, and they want to be the ones to set the pace of how it's presented. To them, it's more than business. It's their reason for living and breathing, it's art. You don't rush someone's art.

"Come, we start here in the kitchen."

We follow him through the arched doorway and end up in a large industrial-looking kitchen.

He turns to us with his arms spread out wide. "This is where the magic happens. My lovely wife Teresa and daughter Isabella prepare all the food that we serve our guests. Everything from zeppole to pasta al limone."

I look over at Savannah as she runs her hands along the counter.

"I can't wait to meet them." She smiles genuinely at Giorgio.

He returns it and says, "They will be delighted to meet you, Miss Savannah. Now, let's go out back. Giovanni is waiting for us."

We follow him out the back door, off the porch and down to the beginning of the vineyard. Giovanni is currently inspecting a grape vine. When he looks up and sees Savannah, I notice his eyes open wide in appreciation as a slow smile spreads across his face.

"Wow. Signorina, you look bellisima." He takes her hand and offers a small kiss on her delicate fingers.

Don't punch the fucker. Remember you want his damn business.

He better not do this shit with her all week or I'll rearrange his face.

Savannah's flirtatious giggle makes my blood boil. I glance sharply at Giovanni, but he's still too enamored with my girl to catch my glare.

Okay, fine, she's not my girl—not yet.

"What are you looking at?" Savannah asks him curiously.

"Just checking the grape shoots to see if they're going to bloom soon. I think we have a couple more weeks. Here, I'll show you," he says as he motions for Savannah to join him. "I'm sure Luke already knows how this works."

He looks at me and I nod my head. Of course I fucking know, but I want to be the one to explain it to her. Why? I don't know. It makes sense that the vintner would be the one to teach her about the process, but I don't think I trust this particular one at the moment.

I spend the next hour walking behind them, nodding along and pretending I'm not clocking Giovanni's every move, every hand placement, every leering glance in Savannah's direction.

"Wow, that's so interesting. I had no idea there was that much that went into growing grapes," Savannah says as we walk back to the villa from the vineyard.

Giovanni did most of the talking, spending too much time speaking directly to Savannah. My hands are clenched into fists in my pockets as we continue through rows and rows of grape vines. Normally I'm lost in the magic of a vineyard and the views you get while walking on the rolling hills of Tuscany.

Not today. Today I'm lost in a world of jealousy and rage as I watch a suave Italian man give all his time and attention to the woman I want but can't have.

"We will bring you to our wine cellar in town tomorrow. You will get to see and taste our fabulous wines," Giorgio says.

That part is my favorite; feeling like magic to me. I could live inside a wine cellar.

"I can't wait." Savannah smiles at Giorgio. "You've already made me fall in love with your farm. I'm sure I'll feel the same about your wine."

"Ah. Love and wine, you already realize the two go together so well," Giorgio says to her.

Savannah is fitting in so well with the culture here. Her natural warmth makes her fit right in, like she's a part of the family. That's exactly the way they do business here—it's all about the relationship you form with them.

"Let's retire to the fireplace. It'll warm us right up, and I'm sure the girls are getting dinner ready. You can meet them," Giorgio says, leading us back to the villa.

We're seated in front of the fire, Savannah to my right, so she's closest to the crackling warmth. Two women come out holding wine glasses and a bottle, laughing at something one of them said.

"Ciao," the older one says. She must be Teresa, Giorgio's wife.

Giorgio stands and grabs the bottle from the woman. "La mia bellissima moglie," he says to her.

He plants a big kiss on her lips, and I think I see a hint of a blush on her cheeks at him calling her his beautiful wife.

"Oh, Giorgio," she says. "Non davanti agli ospiti."

Not in front of the guests, she just said. I smile and wave my hand in the air.

"Non nascondere il tuo amore," I say, telling them not to hide their love.

"Savannah, Luke, this is my beautiful wife Teresa, and my equally beautiful daughter Isabella."

Isabella comes forward and gives us each a wine glass. "Ciao," she says.

"Ciao," I reply as I grab the glass from her. "Grazie."

She's a gorgeous woman with long brown hair and olive skin. She's just like the kind of women I would enjoy on my trips to Italy in the past. And yet, her beauty does nothing for me now. Sure, I can subjectively say she's beautiful, but it's nothing compared to Savannah.

"We open the bottle for a toast then let you two enjoy while we prepare a nice welcome dinner," Giorgio says.

After we do a quick toast to salute, they disappear into the kitchen, leaving me and Savannah alone. I shift my body to face her and rest my arm on the back of the couch. She takes a sip of the wine and closes her eyes as she releases a moan.

"This wine is so good," she says then turns to me. "What do you think?"

I'm so lost in her, I'm hardly even thinking about the wine. Instead, my dumb ass is wondering what her lips would taste like with the wine on them. "Beautiful," I whisper.

Her head tilts to the side as she ponders my words. "What do you think of the wine?" She mirrors my decimal as I see her chest rise and fall a bit quicker.

"The wine?" I look down at my glass. "Oh, I haven't tried it yet."

I sniff the wine to open my senses to the aromas that are floating around in my glass and then I take a sip and let it sit on my tongue for a moment before swallowing. It tastes just like the glass I had in Chicago when I first discovered their family's wine.

This wine, called Montepulciano d'Abruzzo, is from the grapes grown right here on this farm in the Abruzzo region of Tuscany. They have a smaller farm run by cousins in the Chianti region where they grow their sangiovese grapes for their Chianti Classico wine.

"It's exactly liked I hoped it would be. Very rich and bold, a strong blackberry note coming through, but not too strong as to overpower it."

I swirl my glass around again before taking another sip, all the while feeling her eyes on me. I look over and whisper, "What are you staring for?"

"Sorry, just didn't realize I could get so turned on listening to a man talk about wine," she says as she mimics a shiver.

My head falls back as a loud laugh follows. I scoot closer to her on the couch and pinch her side, making her giggle.

"I've got more where that came from, princess," I continue as she laughs. "Just say the word and I'll keep going."

"Stop it," she laughs as I lean into her with a smile.

"I like to leave the wine on my tongue for a bit to get a taste of the body," I whisper as my lips graze her ear. "A full-bodied wine will feel intense and strong on your tongue while the light-bodied will feel refreshing."

She leans back, pushing me away, telling me the exact effect I'm having on her. "Seriously, Luke. I'm gonna have to run upstairs and change my underwear if you don't stop it."

My face falls in an instant while she continues to grin at me, not knowing what she just did. How the hell am I supposed to think of anything else but her wet and glistening pussy when she says something like that? If we were alone in this place, I would fall to my knees and find out just how ready for me that pretty pussy of hers is.

"La cena è servita. Dinner is served," Giorgio says as he comes out of the kitchen holding two large dishes. "Follow me. We eat at the big table here."

I stand up and reach my hand out for Savannah. When she takes it, there's an electricity that buzzes between us. As soon as I see Giovanni come out of the kitchen, I move my hand to her lower back, feeling territorial.

Everyone sits down at the table—Teresa and Giorgio at the heads, Savannah and I next to each other, and Isabella and Giovanni opposite us.

"Everything looks and smells incredible," Savannah says as her eyes light up appreciatively at the center of the table.

"Grazie." Isabella smiles at Savannah, then looks at me. "So nice to have you here, Mr. Giannelli." She gives me a big smile, and I return it.

"Please, call me Luke," I tell her.

"Luke," she says to herself, her Italian accent thick.

We dig into the generous portions of delicious food. They made braciole as the main dish, which pairs very well with the wine. The conversation flows naturally at dinner as we talk about everything from the history of their family to how I got into the wine industry. Savannah dazzles them with her gushing about everything they do, from their food to their wine, the beauty of their land and villas.

She has them wrapped around her finger as she tells the story of her first experience with wine as a teenager. Apparently, she found one of her dad's bottles of expensive wine, not knowing that it was worth something, and stole it to bring to a party.

Needless to say, she has them all laughing as she animatedly explains her father's reaction.

"And what did your mother think about all of this?" Teresa asks.

I see Savannah's face fall, only for a second, before she recovers. "My mother passed away when I was three. Cancer."

Teresa's voice breaks as she says, "Oh, bless you, my dear."

You can tell Teresa really feels for Savannah. Everyone at the table does, including myself. I reach for her hand under the table and give it a squeeze.

"It was a long time ago. It's okay," she says, trying to hide that the attention makes her uncomfortable.

"Well, thank you so much for a lovely evening. I think Savannah and I might just retire to our rooms. We have a long day ahead of us tomorrow."

"Can I help you clean up?" Savannah asks as she begins to pick up her plate.

A small smirk takes over my face, knowing what's to come. I've tried to offer my help before, so I know without a doubt that her offer will not be accepted.

"*Assolutamente no*. Absolutely not," Giorgio responds emphatically.

"Come on, let's go." I stand, swallowing a chuckle at how accurate I was, and put my hand out for hers. "Buona notte. Grazie per la cena. Thank you for dinner."

"Buona notte," they all reply together.

I keep Savannah's hand in mine as we walk up the steps together. The warmth of her hand connecting directly to my heart. I rub my chest as I try to dismiss the funny feeling.

A soon as we're standing outside of her room, she starts to release my hand, but instinct has me squeezing harder and pulling her close.

"Are you okay?" I ask softly.

She looks up at me with a puzzled expression. "What do you mean?"

"I noticed you tensed a bit back there when your mother came up. I just wanted to make sure you were okay."

She looks off in the distance as she shrugs. "It's fine."

"Bullshit. Talk to me, princess." I grip her chin and move it so she's looking directly at me again.

She blows out a breath as if releasing the raw emotion she's been holding in. "My whole life I've seen the same pitiful looks when people learn I lost my mom so young." She shrugs her shoulders dismissively. "It's stupid, I know. It's the normal reaction to have sympathy when you find out someone's loved one passed away, but it just makes me feel like... I don't know... they pity me. It was a long time ago, and sure, it makes me sad to think about it, but I've long since come to terms with my reality. Reliving it when other people find out doesn't do me any good. It's stupid, but it's true."

"Don't talk about yourself like that. It's not stupid to feel like that, it's actually perfectly understandable."

She hesitates for a moment. "You think so?"

"Well, I mean, I don't understand exactly what you're feeling, but I get what you're saying. No one likes to feel like that. I'm just trying..." I stumble over my words. I grip the back of my neck and rub it, slightly embarrassed. "Shit, I'm fucking this up, aren't I?"

She lets out a soft giggle. "Not at all."

Silence falls between us as the moment shifts from friendly to something else—something more complicated. My thumb starts to rub circles over her hand, and I watch as she swallows heavily.

My gaze drops from her throat down to her breasts, then back up to her eyes. There's a hopeful glint in them. Does she want me to kiss her?

I feel my body start to lean in on its own accord as I remember the taste of those lips and am once again plagued by the incessant need to know what they would feel like wrapped around my dick.

Fuck, my dick twitches at the thought, bringing me back to reality. I step away as my hand lets go of hers.

She looks down, and I can see the disappointment etched all over her face.

"Good night, princess," I whisper before turning around.

I walk into my room and close the door quickly before I do something stupid. My forehead rests against the door as I pound my fist on it in frustration.

Why is this so damn hard? I hate that I'm not strong enough to resist her.

I've made it through one day here in this romantic setting. Now I just need to make it through five more.

Chapter Sixteen

Savannah

The prolonged anticipation I'm consistently feeling about will he or won't he kiss me is becoming unbearable. I rest my head back against my door and take a deep breath just as a loud bang comes from across the hall, startling me.

I shouldn't go over there to check on him, that much is obvious. But Giorgio did close the rest of the villa for our stay, and the family stays in the villa next door. This means that noise wasn't from another guest. What if something fell and hit Luke?

I look up at the large wooden beams hanging from the ceiling. Oh no! What if one fell off the ceiling and pierced his face like the log scene from Final Destination?

Okay, so maybe that's a bit drastic, but he *could* be hurt.

Not wanting to take any chances, I open my door and take two big leaps to his door where I knock frantically until the door flies open.

I only have a second to breathe a sigh of relief when I see he is safe and doesn't have a log sticking out of his face because he's standing in front of me with his white shirt unbuttoned, his impressive stomach and pecs on full display.

He takes a step toward me. "Savannah, is everything okay?"

I panic as I struggle to string a single thought together, too focused on staring at the ridges of his abs.

"Um, yeah. I'm good. I'm great. Just happy your head doesn't have a huge piece of wood sticking out of it." My mouth moves while my brain yells at me to shut up.

His eyebrows raise in confusion. "Why the hell would my head have a piece of wood sticking out of it? Are you feeling okay?"

Oh, God. He thinks I'm having some kind of psychotic break, doesn't he?

"Yeah, I'm fine." I wave my hand like it's no big deal. "I just heard a loud bang and thought that maybe one of those big wooden beams fell on you, you know, like from Final Destination. But then here you are, nice and safe, healthy, shirt open, muscular, and..."

Shit, Savannah. Stop talking immediately!

His lips turn up in a devilish smirk as he looks down at himself. "Here I am. Shirt opened... safe and sound."

"Ugh, okay. Whatever. I'm glad you're okay. Goodnight," I huff, then spin around and stomp back to my room.

"Goodnight, princess," he calls with a teasing tone.

Too humiliated to respond, I can only hope that I wake up in the morning to find out it was all a bad dream.

Maybe it all *was* a bad dream. We've made it through breakfast, and Luke hasn't said anything about last night. He's probably so embarrassed for me that he's just gonna laugh about it by himself behind closed doors.

I can blame it on the jetlag. I wasn't thinking clearly.

"We're here," Giovanni announces as we park along the street on the outskirts of the hilltop town.

"I'm glad you wore comfortable shoes," Giorgio says as he points down at my Toms. "We have to walk to the top."

My eyes follow his finger as I look at the cobblestone streets that just keep going up and up... and up. I think my throat makes an audible noise when I gulp. My glutes hurt just looking at it.

"Well, at least I'll be burning off those calories from last night," I reply.

Giovanni and Giorgio laugh in unison.

"She's beautiful, and she's funny," Giovanni says with a smile.

I notice Luke tense up at Giovanni's words. If I didn't know better, I would say he's jealous. I may need to explore that today, just to see what kind of reaction I can get out of him.

The walk, or should I say climb, to the top is brutal. I'm panting and sweating, which is not sexy at all. Why the hell do the men look like they've just taken a leisurely stroll around a nice, flat sidewalk? I'm the youngest one here. This might be more embarrassing than getting caught ogling my professor last night just after I told him I thought a ceiling beam might have penetrated his face.

"This is it!" Giorgio states as he turns to me, no doubt realizing I'm still trying to catch my breath. "Ah, people wonder why us Italians live so long with our pasta and pizza. We don't put machinery in to take us to the top of these places. It doesn't matter if it's high, you're walking."

Luke chuckles as I place my hands on my knees. I look up at him, confused by how unaffected he is.

"Why the hell aren't you more tired?" I curse.

"I've been doing this for years. I'm used to it. I may have been like you my first couple times until I learned my lesson and took up running."

"A little heads up would have been nice." I finally stand and manage to follow them inside.

The room I walk into is, naturally, filled with bottles of wine. There are shelves covering every surface of the walls, and tables are scattered around the room, held up by oak barrels.

"This is our tasting room," Giovanni says as he leads us in. "Just around the corner here, we will take you downstairs to the cellar."

He opens the steel door, and we follow him down a winding set of cement stairs. The temperature continuously drops the further we go, reaching its coldest point once we get to the bottom. I tuck my hands into my pockets to try to combat the cold as I survey my surroundings.

The cellar is made entirely out of brick, with wine racks and barrels lining the perimeter of the room.

I stand in awe as the men begin to discuss the wine, throwing around words I've never heard before. It's amazing how much goes into the process of making wine and just how little most people—myself included—know about it.

Luke's business side comes out as he beings to ask them questions. If I thought the professor version of him was sexy, it's nothing compared to businessman Luke. As they talk through things and Giorgio points things out in different barrels around the room, Luke listens intently.

I try to follow, but I know that half the process is going over my head.

"I think it's time we try some vino," Giorgio says as he claps his hands together in excitement. "Come."

We follow him down the line of barrels. As we walk, Luke places a hand on my lower back. My body instantly takes notice, craving more warmth from his touch. Not because it's cold down here but because it just knows his touch could evoke so many pleasurable feelings.

Luke leans in to whisper in my ear. "It's a good thing there's no wooden beams or logs in here to accidentally stab me in the face." He winks then takes the glass offered by Giovanni.

It takes me a second to rebound from his words. He's smirking at me now as he watches me attempt to pick my jaw up off the floor.

"For you," Giovanni says, pulling me out of my own thoughts.

I notice he's been holding out my glass for God knows how long.

"Oh, thank you. Sorry," I say as I take it from his hand.

"This is our brand that is set to be bottled next week. 2021 Chianti Classico Riserva. Made from our vineyard grapes in Chianti."

Giovanni motions for us to step up to the barrel with our cups, and one by one, we place them under the spigot as he twists the top to let the wine pour through.

I wait for everyone to get theirs, and once all of our glasses are full, I follow suit as they lift theirs in the air to cheers.

"Salute," we say in unison.

Shit, I feel like I'm in an Italian mafia family right now. Like we just finished off the enemy and are in our cold dungeon basement, drinking in celebration.

What the hell is with my imagination lately?

Am I still jet-lagged?

I must be.

Once we finish up with the cellar tour, we head back upstairs.

"Fellas, if you don't mind, I'm gonna show this lovely lady around for a bit," Luke says as we step outside.

"Assolutamente. Absolutely," Giorgio replies. "There's much beauty to see."

"I could take her around. I know the many hidden gems here for this bella signora to see." Giovanni steps up to me, tucking a hair behind my ear.

He's rather beautiful himself, and he's made it very clear that he's attracted to me. I wonder if he has any clue that there's *something* going on between Luke and me. If I don't even know what to call it, I'm sure Giovanni hasn't noticed anything.

I'm not sure what to say or do in this situation. I don't want to be rude, but I don't want to ruin Gianelli Family Selections' chances of getting this business by saying no. I don't think Luke would want those types of people in his life, but the question is still bouncing around in my mind.

Before I have time to formulate a response, Luke's hand finds my hip. He pulls me toward him rather aggressively as his hand squeezes me tightly.

"I think I can handle it, Giovanni," Luke bites out. "Thank you so much for your very generous offer."

Giovanni winks at me. "Can't blame a guy for trying. We can meet back at the car in two hours."

Giorgio chuckles off to the side as he watches the entire interaction take place. I have no idea what he's finding so funny about this when I'm feeling terribly uncomfortable at the moment.

Luke takes my hand and directs me down a road in the other direction. We end up walking the street in silence as I take in all the details around me. I keep waiting for him to drop my hand, but he never does.

"Where are we going?" I eventually ask.

He looks down at me. "Do you like sugar?" he asks with a smile.

I raise an eyebrow at him. "Obviously."

"Then I think you'll like where we're going."

"Have you been here before?"

He squeezes my mind as he leads us down another street. "Many times. There's a family-owned vineyard not far from here that we do business with."

Every time he mentions something like that, I just can't imagine the life he's lived already. I want to know all about it—about him.

"Here we go."

We stop in front of the cutest bakery, with tables sitting outside and colorful flowerpots lining the windows.

"I'm in trouble," I say as we step inside, and I'm hit with the sugary sweet aroma.

"I'll help you work off the calories tonight if you need me to. I'd be willing to take one for the team."

I let go of his hand and shove him playfully. "Watch yourself, mister."

He wraps his arm around my neck and brings his lips to my ear to whisper, "Don't think I didn't see you checking me out last night. You're lucky I was able to keep my hands to myself. But princess, I can't promise the same if I ever catch you looking at me like that again."

As if the proximity of our bodies didn't already have me shivering, I squeeze my legs together on instinct at his words, trying to fight off the reaction he's evoking in me. Being the man that he is, it doesn't go unnoticed.

He lets out a literal groan, then backs away from me. Like he was so tortured knowing what he did to me, his only option—apart from taking me right here—was to let it out with a groan.

"Buon pomeriggio. Come posso aiutarla? Good afternoon. How can I help you?" the young lady at the counter says to Luke.

The look she's giving him makes it pretty obvious that she appreciates what she's seeing. Luke is completely oblivious to the reaction he garners wherever he goes—both from every student in our lecture and every woman we've passed in Italy. That, or he's so used to it he doesn't even react anymore.

I'm not used to it, and I'm trying to find out how to refrain from marking my territory. Unable to stop myself, I walk up to him and wrap my arm around him. He looks down at me with a raised eyebrow, slightly intrigued.

"Buno pomeriggio," I respond, mimicking her. That was one phrase I memorized before I came. "What would you like, babe?"

Luke gives me a knowing smirk, then bites his lip in an effort to conceal it. Dammit, he knows I'm jealous, and apparently, he's enjoying it.

"We'll get due sfogliatelle e due cannoli," Luke orders as he wraps his arm around me.

After she places the pastries in a bag, Luke takes it from her and leads me back outside.

"So"—he places his arm back around my neck and brings me into his chest—"which would you like to try first... babe?"

I try to shrug him off me, annoyed that he feels the need to rub my jealousy in my face. "Ugh, just give me the damn cannoli."

He goes for the sfogliatelle, lobster tail in America, and we start to walk side by side, enjoying our treat. The ricotta-based filling is amazing, not too sweet, and perfectly light. It's impossible to stop myself from moaning as I continue to eat the pastry, it's *that* good.

I think I hear Luke grumble something next to me that sounds like *fucking Gabe was right,* but I'm too into my cannoli to ask him.

Taking in the views around me and indulging in this sweet treat, I take a second to thoroughly enjoy where I am. I honestly can't believe I'm walking the streets of Montepulciano with this handsome man next to me, enjoying the best pastry I've ever tried.

I take my final bite, and some of the cream slips out of my mouth, coating my lips. Before I can lick it off, Luke grabs my hand and drags me to an alley between two old buildings, away from the crowd. His eyes are dark as he puts his hand on my stomach and gently pushes me until my back hits the wall.

My brain is trying to keep up with the present moment. One second, I'm eating; the next, I'm struggling to take in a breath as I watch Luke step into my space. He puts his hand on my face, tugging my head to the right, and then proceeds to lick the cream off my chin.

I let out a small gasp as he whispers, "Next time something is dripping out of your mouth, it's going to be my cum."

And there goes my underwear, they're drenched.

Just as quickly as I ended up against the wall, I'm dragged away with the yank of his hand. Honestly, I didn't know Luke had such dominance in him. It's hot as hell, and it's going to make staying away from him that much harder.

"Once again, an incredible meal," I say to Teresa and Isabella. "I'm so grateful for your wonderful hospitality."

When they stand to clear the table, I stand up and start to pick up whatever I can.

"No, no... We can get this." Teresa tries to wave me off.

"I insist. I can't just sit here and watch you slave over preparing a meal and then do *all* the dishes. Please, let me help."

Thankfully, Teresa caves and lets me bring some dirty dishes back to the kitchen.

"So, what's it like having Luke as a professor?" Isabella asks as I begin to hand her dishes as she rinses them and places them in the dishwasher.

"It's great. He's very passionate about his work, and he makes sure to deliver that same enthusiasm when he's teaching."

"And he's very handsome," she whispers to me. "I'd go to college if men like him were teaching."

I tuck my hair behind my ear nervously. "Oh, I, um... Yeah, he's okay."

"Oooh, you like *like* him," she says with a sigh. "I guess I'll back off if that's the case."

"What? No. No, why would you say that?" I stammer.

"Him being handsome is just obvious. It's not up for debate. You fumble over your words, then tell me he's *okay*," she mimics me in her Italian accent, tutting at me. "No, you're trying to hide something."

I'm momentarily frozen at her ability to see through me. "Oh gosh, I'm not sure what to say. I didn't think I was being so overt," I say, and then it hits me what she said. "Wait... what do you mean you'll back off?"

She laughs a loud, infectious laugh. "It gets boring out here in the country with the same old people day in and day out. If you weren't so obviously hung up on him, I'd be taking my chances."

Despite her admitting her attraction to Luke, I think I like her. She's fun, carefree, and easy to be around.

"You might as well go for it," I tell her with a smile. "He won't do anything with me because I'm his student."

"You hear this, Mamma?" Isabella shouts over her shoulder to Teresa. "Luke won't touch Savannah because she's his student."

I'm expecting Teresa to turn my way with a look of disgust. Instead, she keeps her eyes on the counters as she continues scrubbing them. "You silly Americans."

I look back at Isabella, surprised.

She just laughs at me. "We don't put so many restrictions on love. In Italy, love is love. That is all that matters, not the rules. Is he the one grading your papers?"

"Well, no, his TA does that, I think. But it's still a conflict of interest."

She just shrugs like it's no big deal and looks at me with wide eyes as if a lightbulb has just gone off for her. "I say we make him crazy."

I'm not sure exactly what she's talking about, but it seems like she's already got a plan.

Chapter Seventeen

Savannah

Teresa hands me a bottle of wine and shoos me out of the room.

"Go, bellisima. Go tell Giovanni to open," she says with a knowing smile to Isabella.

I walk back outside to the beautiful patio with string lights hung over the wood pergola and vines growing throughout the trellises. The sun is setting, and the view of the rolling hills in the background makes my heart flutter.

Luke and Giorgio are talking, but as soon as I step outside, Luke turns to me and smiles. I grin back, then walk over to Giovanni, Luke's eyes growing narrow as they follow my path.

"Your mother asked me to bring this to you." I hand the bottle to Giovanni.

His charming smile comes out. "Ah, I see they want to spoil our guests. They must think you're very special. This is one of our best wines. Not many bottles were made."

I feel honored that they're willing to waste one of the bottles on me. I'm nobody in this world of wine enthusiasts.

"I'll be right back, bella ragazza," he tells me. "I will get the wine opener."

Just as he walks away, Luke comes to stand next to me. "What's going on?" he asks.

"What? Nothing. Teresa and Isabella asked me to give Giovanni a bottle to open for us. I guess it's a special wine. I'm excited to try it."

"Looks like you've just charmed all of them here, even the women."

I'm not sure how to take that comment, if it's a compliment or a warning. Was I supposed to be more professional, more stiff? I thought I was taking cues from Luke, but now I'm worried I'm messing up the deal somehow.

Isabella and Giovanni are standing in the doorway, both smiling in my direction. Isabella looks at me, and Giovanni nods his head in understanding as she speaks, then winks at me.

Giovanni begins stalking in my direction and hands me a glass as soon as he reaches me. "Here you go bellisima." When his arm wraps around my waist and brings me to his side, I'm a little taken aback.

"You want your professor to get jealous, you leave it to me, beautiful," he whispers.

Isabella is leaning against the doorway with her arms crossed over her chest and a big smile on her face. I don't know whether to thank her or tell her off. I didn't exactly agree to this, and if it only ends up pissing Luke off and making him pull away from me, I'm not going to appreciate the idea. But on the other hand... I like seeing Luke's jealous side.

"Take a sip," he says a bit louder, and I follow his instructions. He then grabs my chin with his thumb and pointer finger, dragging his thumb up to my bottom lip and pulling on it. "What do you think?"

When I turn my head, Luke looks like I've never seen him before. Fists clenched tightly at his sides, eyes darker than I thought possible, and brows pulled in tight. I think he's going to say something, but he storms toward the villa instead.

"That was easier than I thought. You've got the man wound tight," Giovanni chuckles. "Give it a minute, then go in after him."

With that, he walks away toward the family villa. Isabella and Teresa are finishing up the cleaning outside, and Giorgio has disappeared somewhere. I'm left alone, a bit scared to find out what state Luke is going to be in if I go after him now.

After I don't know how much time has passed, I eventually head up the stairs. When I get to Luke's door, I raise my hand to knock but instead notice the door is cracked open. I can see him by the window, pacing back and forth.

I lightly tap the door to get his attention.

"What are you doing here?" he barks at me.

"Um, you seemed angry when you walked away..." I stammer as I try to figure out what to say. "I just wasn't sure..." I move into the room and close the door, trying to keep the noise level down in case anyone is still downstairs.

"Angry? Yes, Savannah. I'm angry. Do you know why?" He takes a step toward me, clearly irritated, and I shake my head, wanting him to tell me the reason. "I'm angry because Giovanni out there seems to think you're free game to make a move on. And I can't do a damn thing about it because I'm not allowed to claim you."

"Do you want to?" I breathe.

"Do I want to claim you?" he scoffs. "I've wanted to make you mine since the moment I saw you walk into my classroom. It's all I've thought about since we've met, dammit! It's all I want," he says as he closes the distance between us. "But I can't. Not yet. So, until that time comes, I'm stuck watching men like frickin' Giovanni put their hands on what's mine."

"I am yours," I whisper. "I'm yours to have whenever you want me."

My words are getting tangled up in my head. What I'm trying to say is I'm going to be right here waiting for him as soon as the semester is over, but before I can clarify, his lips are on mine.

There's an urgency behind this kiss, like if he stops, he'll lose me forever, and I feel it down to my bones. He pulls away for a second to change angles, grabbing my head and slamming his lips back down. I match the intensity, getting on my toes to mesh myself further against him.

He groans, then takes my arms and brings them around his neck. His hands proceed to move down my back slowly until he reaches my ass, grabbing my cheeks and pulling me into him. His dick is stiff in his pants, and we both groan this time.

When he pulls away, we try to catch our breath together. The only noises I hear are the ones from our heavy panting. His eyes glance behind me, and something seems to occur to him in that moment, like he just thought of something.

He nods his head in the direction behind me. "Remember our word search game?"

I turn my head, arms still wrapped around his neck, and see a huge mirror hanging on the wall. It's about the size of the door and goes down to the ground.

"Katoptronophilia," I say as my eyes remain on the mirror.

I can see him give a small smirk, and then he turns me around to face it.

"Lift your arms up, princess," he whispers in my ear, all the while looking at me through the mirror. "We're going to test this out."

I do as I'm told as the dominant man I got a glimpse of earlier makes an appearance. He slides my sweater up over my head. My black lace bra and jeans are the only things left. We both watch as his hands come up to my breasts and grip them. His large hands massaging my breasts is a different kind of pleasure than I've ever experienced. When his thumb and finger pinch my nipples with a bit of force, I let out a cry at the brief moment of pain.

His hands trail down my stomach. He unbuttons my jeans, and then the sound of my zipper being dragged down echoes throughout the tiled room. Once he pulls my jeans down my legs and I kick them off, I'm left standing in just my bra and underwear. Thankfully I had enough sense to wear a matching pair today.

Call me crazy, but when in Italy, you dress like anything can happen.

His hand moves around my stomach as he drags his nose from my neck up to my cheek. "Let's see what it looks like when my hand disappears into your panties. I'm dying to know if you're as affected by this as I am."

We both watch as his hand dips below the line of black. My heart is racing out of my chest knowing where he's headed, in disbelief that this is really happening. The added element of both our eyes strained on where his hand is going makes the moment feel so much more intense.

His middle finger hits the tip of my clit, and my head falls back against his chest. I'm so sensitive it feels like this could be all it takes for me to lose control.

His entire body stiffens and freezes, making me lift my head back up. "What's wrong?" I hesitate, terrified he's going to say we shouldn't be doing this.

"This only works if you're looking in the mirror. If I have to say it again, you'll be sorry," he growls, then slides his fingers down into my folds. His words have me leaking and he must feel it because he lets out a guttural noise. "You like it when I talk like that, don't you, princess? Look at how sexy it is seeing my hand disappear into your panties. Let's see what it looks like when it rubs circles all over your clit."

He brings his fingers up and starts to move in a slow, deliberate circular motion. Instead of watching his hands, I get lost in his eyes. They hold mine with such intensity, I'm afraid to look away and lose the connection.

My jaw falls slack when I feel my orgasm building, but he pulls his hand away quickly.

"Not yet, baby," he tells me.

He pulls my underwear down my legs slowly and then starts to unbuckle his pants. He looks at me through the mirror, all the while my eyes are trained on his body as he undresses down to his boxers. I swallow my appreciation for the man's impeccable body.

"I need to see this pussy again, in person this time. Sit down on the floor and spread those legs, princess. Right. In. Front. Of. The. Mirror."

Shit, I'm a little nervous. Has anyone ever looked at themselves up close like that, let alone with their crush experiencing it with them for the first time? I obey his command despite my reservations, deciding to put my full trust in him.

Once I'm seated on the floor, I look up at him and he nods his head for me to continue. I spread my legs apart and look in the mirror. I'm slick and wet from what this man is doing to me.

He surprises me by taking a seat behind me and spreading his legs behind mine.

"Lean back, princess," he whispers in my ear.

When I do, it gives us a better angle to see all of me. We're both staring down at my pussy, and it's not scary at all. It's the most intimate, sexiest thing I've ever done with someone.

"Fucking perfect," he says, reaching down. "I need to see my fingers disappear inside of it."

He takes two fingers and starts to push them inside of me, then curls them and hits the perfect spot. The sensations combined with the image is almost overwhelming.

"Wow," I breathe.

"Look how incredible this looks."

We both watch in fascination as his fingers continue the movement in and out. When he slides them up to my clit and starts rubbing circles again, I can feel myself on the edge of losing it.

"Shit, I'm going to come," I tell him.

"Fuck yeah, princess. Keep your eyes open. Watch yourself come," he demands.

And I listen. Even when everything in me wants to close my eyes, I keep them open and watch myself come undone. I watch as I see my muscles clench and spasm around his fingers.

Both of our jaws are slack the entire time we take it all in through the mirror.

When it's over, I lean my head back on his chest and look up at him just as he leans down and kisses me softly. I feel his hard length on my back and reach behind me and wrap my hand around his length.

Luke groans. "What are you doing?"

"What I've wanted to do for a long time," I admit. "Are you clean?" He nods at me. "I am too, and I'm on birth control." I put my hands on the floor and lift myself up.

"Princess, fuck," he starts but drifts off as I slide myself down until I'm seated on him. "Ah, damn!"

He puts his hands on my waist and helps me back up as I drag along his length. Watching his dick appear inch by inch in the mirror, now glistening in my arousal, the sight is indescribable.

"Look at my dick coated in you. Fuck, this is the hottest thing I've ever seen." He tightens his grip on me and slams me down *hard*.

"Ahhh," I scream, not able to hold back.

We do this a couple of times slowly until we get a rhythm and then the pace picks up and sweat starts to trickle down my back. I feel his tongue lick it off my back like the caveman he is right now.

"Fuck. You're so damn tight."

"I'm close," I stutter as I continue to bounce up and down on him.

He lifts me off him then stands up and reaches his hand down. He helps me up off the ground then brings his lips down to mine as he guides me to the bed.

He lies me down gently but makes no move to crawl on top of me. The prolonged anticipation of his next move is almost unbearable. Slow and seductively, his gaze slides downward as his eyes rake my body.

The mere touch of his hand on my knee sends shivers through my body. He must notice and offers me a small smile then continues running his fingers from my knee to my hip then over to my pelvis. They graze over my clit.

With his other hand, he pushes my feet to the edge of the bed and spreads my legs far apart.

"You. Are. Stunning," he says to me with adoration in his tone.

He leans forward, hands on the side of my face, then pulls himself onto the bed as his knees straddle me. Slowly, he lies down on top of me.

His lips reclaim mine. Though this time, the kiss is slow, thoughtful as he pushes himself back inside of me.

The pace is slow, feeling each ridged edge of him as he pulls out. I caress the length of his back as he continues to guide himself in and out.

He starts to go faster, harder as our kisses turn urgent. Then he pushes off the bed with his hands until he is on his knees. He grabs my thighs and pulls me closer to him then starts to fuck me in this position.

"Fuck, yea. I love watching your pussy take my dick like this," he says.

My hand acts on its own and moves to my clit. I start to rub circles over my clit.

"Shit, baby. That's so hot," he tells me. "Keep touching yourself."

He starts to fuck me harder than I think I've ever gotten it before. The sheer force is so intense that I wonder if the bed is going to break.

Thank goodness we are the only ones here because the screams coming out of me are wild.

"I wanna fucking cum all over you," he says as he stares down at our connection.

"Yes!" I shout in agreement. "I want that too. I want to be covered with your cum."

Those words set me off as I soar high until the peak of delight is finally reached and my body starts to squeeze all around him. He pounds on me a few more times through my orgasm then pulls out and pumps his hand over himself.

Thick white ropes of cum start to hit me. First on my pussy, then my thighs, my stomach, and finally my breasts as he leans forward to mark me everywhere.

We are both silent as we look down at my body which is now covered in his cum. It's so hot but also feels very intimate.

"Holy. Shit," he whispers. He falls to my side, and I can't help but laugh as he struggles to catch his breath.

"I'm so freakin' thankful for that word search game," he says.

My body shakes as a giggle falls out, slowly tapering off until silence falls, both our brains working overtime. All these questions start to come through, and I decide to just get it over with and ask him.

"What does this mean for us?" I whisper.

He lets out a long sigh as his hand comes up to rest on my stomach. "I don't know. Clearly I can't resist you in this close proximity. Maybe I just need to step down as the professor."

"What? No, you can't do that!" I exclaim.

"Well, I can't be your professor and be sleeping with you."

I lean up onto my elbows and look down at him. "Have you ever seen the show Friends?"

His eyebrows draw together in confusion. "What? You want to talk about a show right now?"

I ignore him and continue. "Anyway, there's this scene where Monica and Chandler have sex in London. They don't want to ruin their friendship, so they make a pact, sex can only happen in London. When they get back to New York, no sex."

"What are you saying, princess?"

"I'm saying that we should do the same. It doesn't count in Italy. I mean, come on, it's *Italy*. We didn't stand a chance. But when we get back home, no sex until the semester is over and you're not my professor. Rebecca is the one who grades all the papers anyway, right?"

"First Final Destination, now Friends," he mutters, but it looks like he's considering my words. "Technically, yes, she is the one giving the grades. I just read through them and have the final say."

"Sooo, instead of having a say, just don't change my grade."

"Are you saying I get to fuck you as much as I want on this trip?"

Chapter Eighteen

Luke

I open my eyes as a tiny crack in the wooden blinds casts light directly into my eyes. My body is sore. I try to rack my brain for what could be the cause, until I look over and see a beautiful body sleeping soundly next to me.

Savannah.

I smile, remembering I earned every bit of my soreness.

She's a bit of a spitfire in bed. After she convinced me of her plan to only sleep together in Italy, or "Monica and Chandler it" as she calls it, we had another round where she showed me what she can really do when she's on top in bed. That is, until I wanted control back. I suppose that's where my aching muscles come from.

Totally worth it.

After we worked up a sweat, she joined me in my shower. I don't think either of us lasted very long after that before we fell asleep.

I take the opportunity to take her in while she's sleeping, with no one else around us to make me feel dirty or morally flawed.

To someone on the outside, they may see me as a man taking advantage of a younger woman. To me, she's so much more than her beauty. From the moment she first spoke in my class and as

I got to know her, I could tell there was more to her than what meets the eye.

I'm drawn to her for something deeper, something that I can't quite put my finger on. There's this magnetic force when I'm around her that pulls me in despite my best efforts to push away.

We only have two days left in Italy, so I know I need to spend some time this morning ironing out the deal with Giorgio.

I spoke with him briefly after dinner last night. I can tell I've gotten him to trust me, to understand that my desire to sell his wine is because of more than just money, which is exactly what most Italians look for in a business deal. It's a world of difference from making a deal in America. Those are done in the boardroom with numbers and spreadsheets and incessant talks of money.

Knowing I need to get a start on the day, I decide to let Savannah keep sleeping. I kiss her shoulder and sneak away, hoping she won't be upset I'm gone when she wakes up.

When I go downstairs, I find Giorgio inspecting his grapes while singing to himself.

"Buongiorno, Giorgio," I say with a smile, matching his mood.

His grin meets his eyes when he sees me. "Buongiorno, Luke."

"Looks like these are coming along great." I bend over to inspect the vines with him. "You think you will have a good harvest this year?"

He does the sign of the cross. "God willing."

"I really would love to do business with you, Giorgio. Your wine is incredible, of course. But coming here, I can see it's more than that. Your family puts their life and love into it, and I want to share that with the world."

He remains silent for a while. "When we spoke over the phone, I thought you were like most American businessmen, someone who only cared about the money. I'm happy to say spending this time with you has changed my mind. You and Savannah are both lovely. I would be honored to do business with you."

He extends his hand, and I shake it. Of course, I'm happy about landing this deal, but I appreciate his kind words more. Giorgio is a stand-up man, and I'm honored that he can see there's more to me than just someone looking to cut a deal.

We walk along the vines in silence, enjoying how peaceful it is out here. I can imagine this man's blood pressure is phenomenal if he gets to spend his days like this.

"Is Savannah awake yet?" he asks, breaking the silence.

"No, she's sound asleep," I say before thinking better of it. I clear my throat. "I mean, I don't know. I haven't seen her around."

He starts to laugh at my obvious discomfort. "Ah, I see. She is very beautiful. I noticed the way you two looked at each other from the moment you arrived."

"She's my student."

"Non importante. Life is short. At the end of it, those details don't matter. What matters is that you follow your heart."

Only Giorgio can make it sound so simple. I shake my head, knowing it's not.

"Colazione, signore," Teresa shouts from the porch.

"Breakfast. Best not to keep the lady waiting," Giorgio says, turning around immediately.

"Sounds like you have experience with making her wait."

"You learn fast when you get married."

I chuckle as we walk quickly back to the villa.

When we enter the main dining area, I see Savannah laughing with Isabella, and my chest immediately feels strange, lighter somehow. Her eyes meet mine across the room, and my mouth lifts up in an appreciative smile as her face mirrors mine.

I do my best to keep my hands to myself during breakfast, but my palm keeps running up her leg on its own accord. I admit I start to get carried away, inching dangerously close to her pussy, testing her limits. She swats my hand away several times, but I'm not sorry. If I only get her in Italy, I'm taking full advantage.

When we're finished, I ask Giorgio if I would be able to borrow one of his cars and spend the day with Savannah. He gives me the keys without hesitation and practically shoves us out the door, telling us to enjoy the countryside.

"Where are we going?" she asks excitedly as we pull away.

"It's a bit of a drive. A little over an hour, but I think it'll be worth it," I tell her.

"Okay. Where is it?" she asks impatiently.

I look over her with a raised eyebrow. "It's a surprise."

She leans her head back against the seat and sighs. "That's not very nice."

"I never said I was a nice person, bella mia," I say in my best Italian accent.

Her jaw falls, and she folds her arms across her chest, ignoring my comment.

I don't have to think much about directions as I drive on the highway, knowing our destination is a straight shot from here.

Her eyes keep glancing my way, but her pouty face remains in place, which makes me think she doesn't like surprises. I smile to myself at that, finding amusement in being able to rile her up so easily.

"What's so funny?" she asks.

I shrug. "Nothing."

She releases a huff, then looks me up and down. Her hand rests on my knee, an odd display of affection for the moment, until she creeps up my thigh and grips my length. Her hand wraps around me and squeezes, my dick instantly taking notice and hardening at the contact.

I look over at her. "What the hell are you doing?"

She lifts her eyebrows suggestively. "Only the same thing you tried to do to me this morning at breakfast. And now you won't even tell me where we're going. You aren't the only one who gets to have fun on this trip."

Her hand moves up and down my hardening length, making my hands grip the steering wheel in a vice grip.

"Fuck, Savannah. Cut it out," I growl.

My command has the opposite effect, only seeming to spur her on as she unzips my jeans and pulls my dick out of my pants, stroking up and down slowly.

"Dammit, princess. I'm serious," I warn her.

"What are you going to do? Are you going to stop me?" she asks as she tightens her grip and runs her thumb over my tip.

I look at her, knowing she's got me there because *hell no,* I'm not going to stop her. The most beautiful woman I've ever met has her hand wrapped around me as I cruise down a highway in Italy. I think any other man would punch me if they found out I actually stopped her.

Now it's my turn to throw my head back against the seat in frustration. "No."

I do my best to focus on the road, knowing that my first priority is this woman's safety.

She leans over the seat, and as soon as her mouth wraps around my dick, I let out a loud groan. "Fuck. You're full of surprises."

She looks up at me with fluttering eyes while her mouth is filled with my cock. It's damn well the sexiest thing I've ever seen.

Her lips are suctioned around me with such force I think I may pass out from how good it feels. She starts to work up and down my length, her tongue gliding along with her. When she pops off me, she peers up and smiles.

"Your dick is really thick. I think my jaw might hurt after this."

Those are her only words before she wraps those pretty pink lips back around me. When she starts to really pump up and down, I wrap my hand in her hair and squeeze, encouraging her to keep doing what she's doing.

"Fuck, just like that."

I'm a mess of dirty words and crazy noises as she brings me to the edge. Once I'm there, I use her hair like she's my puppet and work her how I want her.

She groans at my control which is when I lose it and shoot into her mouth. My entire body feels like it's floating on a cloud when she pulls away and situates herself in her seat like nothing happened.

"You'll pay for that," I tell her.

"We'll see about that," she replies.

If she's intimidated or scared by my warning, she doesn't show it. Although, if I think about it, what the hell am I complaining about? Despite being terrified of crashing and putting her in harm's way, it was fucking incredible.

Some girls have given up when they see how thick I am, but not Savannah. She took it like a champ, almost like she was even excited by it.

As we get closer to, I decide it might be time to tell her where we're going. With all the amazing Tuscan hills we've seen since we've been here, I thought she might appreciate seeing something a bit different.

"You ready to find out where we're going?" I ask, glancing over at her, and her smile is the only answer I need. "Ever seen Michelangelo's David up close?" I say, hoping she understands my hint.

She straightens herself in her seat as a look of excitement flashes across her face. "Florence?"

I nod my head, confirming her question with a grin, and she squeals.

"We're gonna start with seeing David and then go to the Cathedral. After that, I managed to score us a reservation at the amazing La Giostra."

She reaches over and kisses my cheek. "Thank you."

I feel blissfully alive and happy.

I don't want to analyze what that small gesture makes me feel. I'm pretty sure it's deeper and more powerful than I've ever experienced.

As soon as we step into the gallery, we are instantly flooded with crowds of people. I grab her hand and lead her down the halls as we look at hundreds of sculptures and paintings. It's nice doing this with someone by my side, someone to whisper something to and laugh with.

If Marcus were here, he would just tell me he's bored, and Gabe wouldn't step away from work long enough to attend in the first place.

When we walk into the room that houses David, it takes a good twenty minutes to get through the line. At the front, we take in the large sculpture, the sign telling us it's seventeen feet tall. We both crane our necks to get the full view of David, noting the intricacy and perfection of it.

"Wow, the detail is incredible," Savannah whispers. "Look at his hand. You can even see the veins in them."

We stand in awe for several more minutes before she whispers in my ear. "Why's his thing so small?"

I snort, then wrap my arm around her neck and pull her along with me. "I don't know, princess. Maybe it was cold out."

"I'm just saying, if you're going to make everything else about him so grandiose, might as well give him a bigger package."

We leave the gallery crying tears of laughter. I'm discovering that any time spent with Savannah is the most fun I've ever had.

I can't help but steal a kiss outside. It was meant to be a quick one, but her lips are just too addicting. I get lost in them, becoming greedy for more. When I pull away, we're both struggling to catch our breath.

The rest of the day goes by quickly. From exploring the cathedral to having a romantic dinner, it all plays out perfectly. It's late by the time we get back to the vineyard, and I hold her hand as we take the stairs up to our rooms. We stop in the middle, looking between her door and mine. Finally, I make the decision and pull her into my room.

As soon as the door is closed, I crash into her, kissing her like I've wanted to all day. My hands rest on her cheeks as I rub my thumbs along her soft skin, backing her up until we hit the bed, and then lay her down.

We waste no time getting to the point. I work her jeans off while she sheds her top and bra. I stand up, reaching behind my back and pulling my shirt over my head. My jeans are off in seconds, pulling my boxers down with them before I remove the final piece of fabric off her, down her hips and slender legs.

I feel like a man possessed as I stare at Savannah lying there waiting for me. I climb on top of her and lean down to kiss her lips. I start to tease her as I pull slightly away so our lips are barely brushing together, then go back in for more.

I need to taste her nipples. They've been calling for me. I kiss my way down her neck and chest until I get to where I've been dreaming to be.

So far, it's been a crazy ride of unique sexual experiences for us, and don't get me wrong, they've been the best of my life. But right now, I just want it to be me and her together, connecting and taking our time. I want to look in her eyes and really feel it.

After I feel her squirming underneath me, I move down lower until I get to her beautiful pussy.

"How have I not tasted you yet? That seems like a sin," I growl while I spread her legs further apart.

My mouth actually waters at the sight, but tonight is about taking my time. I spread her lips with my thumbs then work her clit with one thumb.

Ever so slightly, I move forward and take one long slow lick from bottom to top.

Fuck, she tastes even better than I imagined. I give her a couple more licks and then I suck her clit.

"Ahhh, shit," she shouts as she pushes her pelvis up into my face.

I can't help but smile while continuing to suck and keep pressure on her clit. I love how she is so damn responsive and confident in bed. It's sexy how she holds nothing back.

I continue flicking and licking until, finally, she unravels, coming all over my tongue. I lick up as much of her juices as I can.

I move back up to her, feeling her release all over my lips. Instead of shying away from kissing me, Savannah grabs my neck and pulls me into her. Knowing she's more than ready for me, I position myself and slide in.

We both moan into each other's mouths at the feeling of coming together like this. It's different this time, like maybe it isn't just for pleasure. It's more, I want to feel close to her in this way, and I know she feels the same.

I pull away and gaze into her eyes, which makes my heart accelerate. I get lost in her stare as I continue to slide in and out of her.

Her pussy starts to squeeze me, which gives me the signal that I need to let go of my own orgasm that I've been fighting off. I've never come inside a woman before, but I can't bear to make this less special by coming on her or the sheets. I want to remain connected the entire time. She must feel the same because her hands grip my hips and hold me inside of her as my release takes over.

We both seem to still be lost in the moment, in each other's eyes, as our bodies take their time recovering.

"Wow," she whispers.

I nod my head, feeling too overwhelmed for words. Instead, I fall down onto her and rest my head on her chest, silently wishing that we could spend forever like this. That reality won't step in and force me to treat her like just another student.

Chapter Nineteen

Savannah

"What are you thinking about?" Luke's voice pulls me out of my trance, realizing I've been looking out the window for a while.

I glance over at him, seeing how his curious eyes hold so much adoration. It makes me want to clutch my chest in response.

"I was just thinking how much I'm going to miss them," I tell him.

"They definitely loved you. I think Giorgio only signed on the dotted line because of you."

I shake my head with a smile. Luke doesn't realize the power he has over people. He's naturally good at making anyone and everyone feel at home and appreciated.

"Even Giovanni?" I tease, earning me a side eye from Luke.

Giovanni told Luke about the plan to get him to crack. I was terrified that he would think I was behind it, but Isabella admitted she was the mastermind. Thankfully, Luke took it all in stride and only minor disbelief, shaking Giovanni's hand in the end.

I don't think either of us could regret what happened in Italy. It was too magical, too life altering to regret. I smile briefly, then think about what's to come when we land.

"It's going to be a long five weeks until the semester is over," I tell him.

The mood suddenly changes to a gloomy one as we sit in silence, staring at each other, knowing that as soon as we get off this plane, everything has to change.

"It'll go by faster than you realize," he finally speaks. "In the grand scheme of things, five weeks of abstaining from anything sexual isn't going to be the end of the world. Right?" He looks at me like he's worried I'm going to change my mind about us.

I smile at him, hoping to ease his mind. "I'll take you any way I can get you."

Just as the plane touches down, Luke breaks the rules and un-buckles his seatbelt. I'm expecting one of the stewardesses to say something, but nobody does.

He puts each of his hands on my arm rests and leans down, crashing his lips to mine. His slow, drugging kiss lights up my body before he pulls away too soon.

"I just needed one more kiss to hold me over," he whispers then backs up and sits in his seat.

Within minutes, we are parked and being escorted off the plane. We descend down the stairs, where our luggage is waiting for us at the bottom. Flying commercial after this experience is going to suck.

Luke and I stroll next to each other and walk back to the main entrance. When I stop at the passenger pickup area, he turns around, looking at me strangely.

"What?" I ask.

"Why did you stop?"

"I need to get a car back to my apartment."

"Don't be silly. I parked my car in the long-term parking. I'll drive you home."

Dread instantly fills my insides at the thought of him seeing where I live, knowing it will set him off after that heated spiel he gave me about my safety being his priority.

"No, it's okay. I don't want to inconvenience you," I say.

He doesn't seem to be having it, as my hand is now grasped tightly within his as he drags us in the direction of his car.

"You're being ridiculous. I don't live too far from campus."

Well, I guess that's that. All I can hope is that he doesn't know the streets of Cleveland very well and just thinks it's a run-down area.

We load our things into his fancy car, another glaringly obvious reason why the next hour isn't going to go well and pull out of the parking lot.

He asks for my address and proceeds to type it into his GPS. If he's familiar with the street name, he doesn't show it. I take a deep breath as I try to think of a good explanation for why I live where I live, too stubborn to tell him I refuse to let my dad down by admitting I can't swing the rent and utilities on my own at my old place.

In this moment, I feel like such a weak and immature college student.

It's incredible how quickly reality managed to smack me in the face the second we landed back in America. Almost as if Italy was just a dream. One where I was good enough for such a successful, handsome man. I feel like our age difference has never been more transparent than it is now.

As we inch closer and closer to my apartment, the streets show their wear and tear more and more. Homeless people are on every street corner, and I think I even see a drug deal taking place.

I see him shift in seat, looking a bit uncomfortable as we turn onto my street and the GPS brings him to a stop outside of my apartment.

He pulls up right in front of it and slams the car in park then takes a deep breath.

"Please tell me this isn't seriously where you live?" He turns to me.

I swallow the embarrassment growing inside of me and simply nod my head.

"Who do you live with?" he asks.

Shit, I didn't anticipate that question. I let the silence linger, unwilling to answer his question.

"Dammit, Savannah. Who do you live with?"

I risk a peek at him and see his anger is only growing.

"It's just me and Bailey."

"Do you understand how unsafe this neighborhood is? I'm not one to be overly dramatic, but I can confidently say I wouldn't even feel safe living here. Why are you living here and not on campus?"

"It's complicated."

"Is there something I need to know?" he asks accusingly.

My eyebrows draw together. "What the hell does that mean? I don't know what you're insinuating. My dad just couldn't help out as much with funds this year. He's already paying for my tuition, which isn't cheap, and I didn't want to make him feel bad, so I told him I could handle it on my own. This is all I could afford. It's not a big deal."

I do my best to shake off the image of the two men who cornered me.

"You mean your father doesn't know you live here?" He runs his hand through his hair with frustration. "There's no way he would be okay with this. You can't stay here."

Easy for him to say, like it's that simple for me to find a more affordable place in a better neighborhood.

"I don't have any other options. It's only five more weeks. The lease is monthly, so I'm able to get out as soon as school is over."

He shakes his head as I'm talking. "No. There's no way in hell I'm letting you stay here."

I understand being concerned, or shit, even judging me like I expected, but I didn't expect him to demand I stay somewhere else. It's making me angry that he thinks he has a say in my situation.

"Well, that's not your call to make. My family is in Cincinnati, and I have no one else here to stay with. I'm afraid you're just going to have to get over it." I fold my arms across my chest, feeling like I put him in his place.

"Princess, your safety is always my business. Now, let's go pack some of your things. We'll get the rest tomorrow." He opens his door and gets out.

I get out of the car and quickly follow behind him. "What? I told you I don't have anywhere to go. Luke, you're being stubborn."

"You're staying with me." That's all he says before he's stalking toward the door of my apartment building.

"I can't stay with you."

"Why not?" he calls over his shoulder.

"Well, for one, I have Bailey."

"It's a good thing our dogs seemed to love each other. Vino will be happy to have a temporary roommate."

"What about no sex while we're back here?" I ask.

"I can keep my hands to myself if I know it's for your safety. I have a guest bedroom. There's no reason for you to pass this up."

He's got me there with a guest bedroom, and our dogs can play together while we're gone.

The only thing holding me back is my pride. Reluctantly, I nod my head and walk ahead of him. He follows me up the stairs until we get to my door. Before I open it, I turn to him.

"I need you to just... bite your tongue when we get inside. No comments about the furniture or lack thereof. Just... please."

"I can do that," Luke promises.

We walk into the apartment and I inwardly cringe at the futon and coffee table that cost me next to nothing and that I put together on my own. That's about all that's in the living room.

"Just take a seat. I'll pack my stuff and be right out. We'll need to swing by and pick up Bailey from the family that watches her when I'm out of town."

With that, I disappear into my room. Well, *room* is generous. I have a blow-up mattress and a cheap nightstand. I couldn't afford the delivery of my real mattress, nor could I get one up here all by myself.

I take two large weekend bags and fill them up with as many clothes as I can, my shower supplies, and makeup, and then I pack all of Bailey's things that aren't currently with her at the Martin's.

When I come out, he quickly stands from the futon and grabs my bags from me.

"Thanks," I say. "I'm just going to grab my backpack."

"Is there much more?" he asks.

I shake my head. "Just some kitchen stuff and more clothes."

I can tell he wants to say something, and I'm grateful when he holds it in.

We walk out of the apartment, and it feels nice to know I'll never spend another scary night here again, wondering if those two guys are going to come back. Worrying that they know where I live and are just biding their time to attack again.

I told Luke I needed my car and to just give me his address so I could meet him there after I picked up Bailey. He insisted he follow my path all the way to his place. I think he thought I was a flight risk and might run off, finding somewhere besides his house to go. Honestly, I thought about it.

It's getting dark as we pull up to his house in Shaker Heights, and as I take in the Victorian monstrosity before me, I'm realizing running is exactly what I should have done.

I'm so out of my element here. We took a private jet to Italy, I should have expected his house to be incredible, but I really hadn't given it much thought.

We drive up a long driveway surrounded by bushes, and he opens his garage door before pulling in and parking. I start to head to the top of the driveway, but Luke waves at me as he gets out of his car.

"Park your car next to mine," he tells me.

I'm ready to argue, but his face tells me this is another nonnegotiable for him today. Maybe he's being Mr. Grumpy from jetlag or something.

Either way, I give in and park my car next to his, like we're some kind of happily married couple who just so happen to drive two very different cars.

Bailey is aggressively wagging her tail in the back seat as Luke approaches. He looks in the back window and smiles, which only makes my dog freak out more.

"I'm going to open the door for her. This side door opens to my backyard, and it's all fenced in so she can't run away."

I nod my head, acknowledging that Bailey is going to get spoiled living here. I'll have a depressed dog when I have to bring her back to our reality in five weeks, one that doesn't include a mansion or a dog friend.

I decide to leave my things in my car for the time being. Right now, I need to make sure Bailey minds her manners in this expensive home.

I'm not far behind them but when I get out there, Luke is chasing Bailey around the backyard.

Shit, don't fall in love, Savannah.

Any dog lover knows what I'm talking about. There's something about a sexy man lovin' on your dog that makes your heart beat faster.

Bailey comes barreling at me wagging her tail. "Hi, girl." I squat and give her head scratches.

"I'm going to go say hi to Vino and let her out. My brother said he just left here about an hour ago, but it's crazy how much we can miss our dogs while we're away."

When Luke returns, Vino is at his side until she spots Bailey.

They're playing within an instant as Vino seems to show her new friend around the backyard.

I walk up to Luke on his massive patio with all the bells and whistles. There's even a covered area with a stone fireplace that has a big TV hanging over it. The couches look so warm and inviting, it makes me want to cozy up to the fireplace with a good book and a glass of wine.

"I'm going to bring your stuff in." Luke pulls me from my thoughts. "Just keep an eye on these two. Make sure they don't get into any trouble."

I'm pretty sure they're fine together, and he's just trying to find a way to keep me from insisting I help. I only met his mother briefly, but spending five minutes with Luke is enough to make it clear that she raised this man to treat women with respect.

Ten minutes later, he comes outside holding his cell phone.

"I just ordered some dinner. I figured with all the pasta we've had this past week, a good salad wouldn't hurt."

I place my hand over my stomach. "Thank you. I probably gained five pounds I'll need to work off."

He looks at me sharply. "Don't be ridiculous. You're perfect."

Silence falls between us. I'm not sure how to respond to that now that we're back to just being friends for the time being. He must notice my discomfort because he quickly changes the subject.

"Come on, let me show you around. I already moved your things to the guest bedroom."

With that, we walk into his house through the back door off the patio while our dogs trot in behind us.

I think I instantly fall in love with the interior of the home. It's an incredible mixture of the old woodwork with some contemporary elements and so much detail.

"This woodwork on these railings is incredible. I feel like I'm walking up the grand staircase in the Titanic."

He turns around, looking at me with a faint glint of humor in his eyes. "You and your movies."

"Who said I was saying it in reference to the movie? What if I'm just a big Titanic historian?"

His eyebrows raise suspiciously. "What date did the ship sink?"

I narrow my eyebrows in frustration. Ugh, I wish I knew the answer to shove in his smug face. "Ugh, whatever. Just keep walking."

Luke laughs loudly as he continues climbing the stairs. We walk down a long hallway with several doors on both sides, and when we get to the end of the hall, he opens the door on the right and leads me in.

The room is equally as beautiful as everything else I've seen. Trim on the top of the room that is detailed and ornate. It has a large four-poster bedframe that matches the grandiose style of the room. A white and cream area rug is splayed out underneath the bed, with a white down comforter with cream throw pillows bringing out the accents in the rug.

I see a mirror set in the corner of the room, and all I can think about is what we did in Italy. I feel myself flush hot as my brain plays it back to me. His eyes follow mine, realizing exactly what has me stopped in my tracks.

When Luke turns back to me, his eyes are dark. "We can't," his deep voice echoes through the room.

"I didn't say anything," I whisper.

"You didn't have to."

"Well, shit, I can't just forget about what happened," I tell him. "Moving on, let's just power through this. I think it's the only way we're going to survive," I plead.

He blows out a breath and nods. "So, this is your room. Please make yourself at home, use whatever you'd like. Through this door here," he says as he opens it and flips on the light, "is your bathroom."

I follow him in and almost scream with excitement. It's literally the size of my shitty apartment.

"Holy shit," I whisper. "It's huge."

"It was built to be a backup master bedroom and bath in case whoever bought the house didn't want the master on the first floor."

"Ah, yes, of course. One would naturally build two if they couldn't decide where to put the bedroom."

Luke walks farther into the bathroom and shows me a closet that has towels and every shower or bath product imaginable. He's pointing stuff out to me when we hear our dogs playing behind us in the bedroom, chasing each other in circles. We look at each other and laugh.

"How are we going to be able to separate them at bedtime?" I ask.

He shuts off the light, and we walk back into the room. "It's probably a good thing my bedroom is on a different floor."

There's many *reasons that is a good thing*, I think to myself.

"Well, I'll let you unpack and get settled in. I'm going to go grab a quick shower. I'll let you know when our dinner is here."

I nod. "Just let me know what I owe you for my salad."

He stops at the door. "It's a salad, Savannah. I'm not gonna make you pay me back for it."

"I'm not a charity case," I snap before I can stop myself.

He folds his arms across his chest and leans on the doorframe. "You know, I wouldn't accept money from any guest of mine. It has nothing to do with who you are to me. It's just the manners I was raised with. If you're in my home, I provide the food. I grew up in a big Italian family. No one argues about food with us. You want to call my ma and see what she has to say?"

I laugh at his dare. "No, I believe you. Thank you."

When he's gone, I look around at the room I'll be spending the next month. Bailey is sitting at my feet, looking up at me. I squat down and scratch behind her ears in her favorite spot.

"What do you think of this place?" I ask. She wags her tail faster, indicating she likes it. "I know, it's a lot better—and safer. You won't have to fend off any attackers around here."

I unpack my things and then decide I could use a shower too.

I have this nagging feeling that I should've just insisted I stay at my place. What would the girls think if they knew I was living with Professor Luke?

Chapter Twenty

Luke

"Get it, Vino," I yell as I toss the ball in the backyard, balancing my cup of warm coffee.

I'm standing here frustrated, trying to figure out what the hell I'm supposed to do with Savannah still sleeping upstairs.

It took me forever to get to sleep last night, knowing she was a short walk away. I could slip into her bed, and nobody would know. Nobody but me and my damn subconscious, which would be nagging me for the next five weeks.

Bailey comes running out of the door, dodging me, and heading for Vino.

I turn around to see Savannah, still in her pajamas, walking toward me, and my breath hitches.

"They survived their first night apart," she says with a sleepy smile.

I'm too awestruck by her natural beauty, waking up with no makeup and hair askew. It takes me a second to register her words.

What I want to say is I survived my first night apart from her; that's a much greater accomplishment.

"Together at last," I settle for as I turn back to them playing in the yard.

"Mmm...your coffee smells delicious," she says with her eyes closed.

I don't give it a second thought, and I extend my arm to give her my cup.

"What? No, I didn't mean I wanted yours."

"Take it, I've only had one sip. I'll go make myself another," I tell her. "Please. I'll stand here and hold it in front of you until it gets cold, and neither of us can drink it."

The look on her face tells me she's not amused, but she takes the cup.

"Thank you."

"I'm gonna go make another. We can leave these rascals out here to play for a bit if you want to join me."

"Sure."

We get back into the kitchen, and she takes a seat at the island while I grab another cup.

"How did you sleep?" I ask.

"Not bad for being in a strange place. It was nice to have Bailey back with me. She always gives me comfort. I hope you don't mind," she pauses, seeming reluctant to finish. "I let her sleep in the bed with me. She always has, so I was afraid she would bark all night if I didn't let her."

I smile as I grab my freshly brewed cup and rest on the opposite side of the island. "I think it's animal cruelty to make your dog sleep anywhere else."

That gets a laugh out of her. "I don't know if I'd go that far, but I'm happy to know you agree with me."

"So, I was thinking we get the rest of your things this morning," I tell her. "Then you can let your landlord know that you no longer need your lease."

She sighs. "Are you sure about this?"

"I'm sure that I'm not letting you live there alone."

After breakfast, we get into my car and start to make our way back to her apartment. She begins to fidget in her seat.

"What's wrong?" I ask as I keep my eyes on the road.

I can feel her eyes on me. "Um, I don't think the rest of my things are going to fit in this car. I know I don't have much, like...embarrassingly little compared to you, but I..."

I rest my hand on her leg that she is bouncing up and down.

"Don't do that to yourself. Nothing about your situation is embarrassing. I know I acted like an ass yesterday when I found out, and I'm sorry for that. I was just worried for you. But this isn't anything to be embarrassed about. It's admirable how much you care about your father's happiness. It shows just how big of a heart you have. It's one of the reasons I'm so..." I stop before the anymore words can come out. I quickly recover. "Anyway, my brothers are meeting us there with Marcus's truck and a small trailer they rented.

"What? Your brothers are coming? Oh, my God." She rests her head back on the seat, sounding exasperated. "I don't want them to see where I live, the sad state of my poor, lonely life."

"Savannah. Stop talking about yourself like that. Are we going to need to stand in front of the mirror every morning and do positive affirmations?"

She looks over at me with squinted eyes. "You wouldn't dare make me do something so humiliating."

I chuckle. "I will if you keep talking about yourself like this."

We reach her apartment and Marcus and Gabe are standing next to the trailer, back door open and ready to go.

I can feel the panic coming off Savannah in waves. I hate that she feels this way about herself.

When we step out of the car, she follows behind me like a shy puppy. It's enough to make me reach for her hand and give it a squeeze.

As we walk up to my brothers, Gabe's eyes zero in on my hand that is still holding onto Savannah's.

I may have called them last night and told them some of the details, leaving out the part where we slept together in Italy. Though they aren't dumb, they know this is not your standard relationship with a student. Well, who the hell knows with Marcus. I wouldn't be surprised if he somehow sweet-talked his way into more than one teacher's bed.

"Thanks for coming," I tell them.

"No problem. Nice to see you again, Savannah," Marcus says with a wink.

I give him a look, hopefully signaling to him to back the fuck off. I've never been the jealous type, always finding it humorous when Marcus flirts with my dates. I know he wouldn't jump in and steal them away, he's just a man-whore and serial flirt. But this time there's nothing funny about it.

She smiles. "You too. Thanks so much for helping."

Gabe looks between us then back at Marcus.

"How do you know her?" he asks Marcus.

"She was a server at your wedding, dude. Way to be a dick and not know anything about the people you hired."

Savannah lets out a small laugh.

Marcus is good for breaking the tension. I'm fine with that as long as he stays the hell away from my girl... Well, soon-to-be my girl.

Gabe cringes. "Sorry. I didn't realize."

"Don't worry about it," she smiles. "We're supposed to be invisible to the guests. That's what we're told."

Why does that make me irrationally angry? I want to punch anyone in the face who tells her to make herself invisible.

"Well, should we get started?" Marcus interrupts my train of thought.

We make our way into her apartment. Again, my protective side comes out when I get another glimpse of where she's been living on her own. I know Savannah is self-conscious about anyone else seeing her place. Luckily, Marcus says what we're all thinking, getting rid of any awkwardness.

"Savannah, you're kind of a badass in my mind now that I've seen where you've been slumming it. I like a girl who can hold her own," he says as he and Gabe work on disassembling the futon.

"Make a move on her, and I'll cut off your dick," I growl.

Savannah's head snaps to me. "Luke! That's horrible. He didn't mean it like that. Right, Marcus?"

Marcus shrugs. "You'll never know."

I roll my eyes while Gabe laughs.

"How was the honeymoon?" Savannah asks Gabe, showing how thoughtful she is.

Gabe stops what he's doing and meets her eyes, always the gentleman to show a woman respect. "It was incredible. Thanks for asking. I'm hoping we made a baby."

"Aww. You two will no doubt make gorgeous babies," she tells him.

I think I see Gabe blush slightly at her words. The man is a completely different person now that he's found Alexis. What was once a bitter, heartbroken shell of a man is now a happy, mushy guy who loves the women in his life.

They brought a couple of boxes for Savannah to throw her miscellaneous items into. While she works on filling them, the guys help me move the heavier things to the trailer.

We have the entire place packed up within the hour.

My brothers follow us to my house where we unload her things into the third section of my garage.

While we finish up, Savannah heads to the backyard with the dogs. I let out an exhausted sigh and shake their hands.

"Thanks for the help. I really do appreciate it on such short notice."

"Anytime, buddy." Marcus slaps my arm.

Gabe looks around, hesitating slightly. "Look, I don't want to be the downer of the group, but I have to say something," he starts. "I'm not going to ask what's going on between you two, I think it's obvious there's something. Just...be careful. I don't want you to get in trouble or worse, get her in trouble with the school."

I nod my head, hating that he even has to worry about something like that. "We don't plan on doing anything until school is over, but I appreciate your concern."

He takes a noticeable breath, like he can relax knowing we aren't having sex. There's no need to admit what happened already between her and I.

After I send them off, I walk into the backyard to find the dogs draped on top of Savannah as she lies on the patio couch under the wooden awning.

"Look at you," I say as I walk up to her, gently lifting her feet and placing them on my lap after sitting. "Are you the dog whisperer?"

She smiles. "It's like heaven out here. The trees, the breeze from the fan, the doggies."

I look over at her, wishing I could lean down and kiss her lips.

"Are you hungry for lunch?"

"I could eat."

"I can order something or make something. I'll need to go grocery shopping first. There's no food in the house."

Her eyes light up with excitement. "I'll go grocery shopping with you."

I lift an eyebrow at her. "You seem excited about that."

"I love grocery shopping," she says. She claps her hands as she sits up, the dogs hopping off her to allow her the room to move. "Let's go."

We get to the store and she is already several steps ahead of me pushing the shopping cart. I take a few extra-long strides to catch up with her.

"I'm gonna guess with your little speech last night about paying for your guests that you won't let me pitch in on this."

"You are correct," I tell her.

"You're going to regret that. I'm like a kid in a candy store at the grocery store."

"Have at it, babe."

I follow her as we make our way through the produce, stopping at the peaches to test a few.

"Oh, yeah," she moans. "These are perfect. Peaches are starting to come back in season."

I come up behind her and lean over her shoulder. "Must you moan like that," I whisper in her ear. "It's distracting."

"But," she holds up her peach, "feel it. It's perfect. Soft and ripe. I bet it's so juicy."

I growl. "You don't realize what you're saying right now."

She looks over her shoulder and I see the moment it clicks. "Oh, you're gross. Get your mind out of the gutter."

I chuckle behind her. "I can't help it. The sexiest woman I've ever met is feeling peaches while she moans and talks about their juices."

The rest of the trip is filled with more of the same—playful banter and plenty of laughs. It's the most fun I've ever had at the grocery store. I thought being in Italy with Savannah was dangerous. Turns out, doing everyday things with her here in Cleveland is more dangerous for my heart. It's been a day and I already know my feelings for her are growing.

Chapter Twenty-One

Savannah

"Okay, lay it on me. How many hot Italian men did you meet out there?" Shannon asks over her coffee cup.

We all agreed to meet at the coffee shop on campus before class. I haven't even taken my first sip before Shannon goes straight for the hot Italians.

I laugh. "It was actually a lot of time spent on the family farm. Although, their son, Giovanni, was quite the looker."

"Shut up. Did you sleep with him?" she asks.

All three girls are looking at me wide-eyed.

"No! I couldn't do that. Luke...Professor Luke was there to win them over for business. I think that would be like a conflict of interest or something."

"Okay, forget about her and her hormones. What was it like? Is Tuscany as amazing as it seems in pictures?" Tricia asks.

With my hand to my heart, I let out a sigh of wonder. "It was better. More beautiful than any picture you've ever seen, times a hundred. The hills— they just go on forever. And the towns, they're so old but preserved. And the people, they just all have this energy about them. It's calming, and it makes you feel that way too."

"It sounds amazing," Aubrey says.

"And what about Professor Luke?" Shannon asks as she wiggles her eyebrows. "What was it like being so close to him all that time?"

"Seriously, Shannon?" Aubrey interrupts.

"What?" she defends. "We've all commented about how gorgeous he is. That's a valid question to ask."

"Maybe, eventually, but she was in Italy. You'd think you would start by asking about the food and the wine," Tricia joins in.

My body starts to sweat as they go back and forth. I hate this lying, especially to my closest friends. But I can't jeopardize Luke's trust by telling them. Instead, I try to divert the conversation.

"The food was heavenly. I mean seriously...it's like there's some kind of magic in their soil that makes everything that they grow taste better. Learning about the winemaking process was so fascinating. There's so much to it that I had no idea about," I tell them.

We get lost in conversation when Tricia points out that we need to get to class.

We're sitting in our usual seats in the front when Luke walks in.

"Good morning, class" he begins. "I hope everybody enjoyed their spring break."

His eyes meet mine and he smirks. Last night was amazing. We cooked dinner together, a large grilled shrimp salad. We sat outside while the dogs played, and we enjoyed our food. It was perfect.

Aside from it being nearly impossible to turn off my sexual attraction to him, it's surprisingly easy to be around him. There's no awkwardness. We fit together so easy.

He had me cracking up as he told me stories about his family with so much animation. It's a side that I don't think many people see of him, and I'm soaking in every second that he reveals his true self to me.

Since the jetlag was starting to set in, both of us went to bed right after dinner. I'm feeling mildly better today, only slightly dragging.

Luke starts to go over our final assignment. We're going to get assigned to our international student this week. I'm excited to find out where my student lives.

Ever the professional, Luke keeps his eyes focused on everybody else. Maybe we can do this. Like he already said, he doesn't give the letter grade, Rebecca does.

Most of class is otherwise uneventful, apart from a few stolen glances my way from Luke. When he spots me, he tries his best to hide the smile that wants to creep up. I love that just the sight of me does that to him. It makes me feel so...loved. I know we haven't even begun to date, so the idea of love is crazy, but I just don't know how else to label these growing feelings.

Class ends and once again, the girls are inviting me to come hang out, and I decline. They don't even seem fazed by it anymore, they just nod their heads and walk away with promises to see me again next class. I don't know if I feel relieved by their lack of surprise, or guilty.

Both, I decide.

Luke told me this morning he didn't want me walking to my car alone at this time of day, so I start for his desk as he packs his things. All the students have filed out of the room. Once again, it's me, Luke, and Rebecca left in the room.

Her eyes hold mine, giving me a strange feeling. Instead of walking up to him, I move passed his desk and head for the exit. I turn back around and both sets of eyes are on me. I don't know what the hell he wants me to do. I can't wait for him with Rebecca on his ass.

Not knowing what else to do, I continue out the door and head to my car.

Chapter Twenty-Two

Luke

"Looks like someone wants more alone time with you," Rebecca says, pulling my eyes away from Savannah. "You'd think she got enough of it in Italy."

I'm not sure what she wants me to say back to that. She's been making strange comments to me all semester, telling me when she's free, like she's waiting for me to make a move.

You'd think if I haven't taken the bait yet, she'd take the hint that I'm not interested.

"Italy was busy. The family that hosted us were very accommodating, and always with us." I barely look up, feeling annoyed that she always seems to pick on Savannah just because she's come to my desk a couple of times after class. It's not out of the ordinary for a student to approach me after class with questions, male or female.

So why is she singling out Savannah, does she sense something between us?

"I wish I could've gone with you. I'm sure it was annoying to babysit a student," she says.

"I wouldn't call it babysitting when the student is an adult." I throw the last of my papers into my briefcase. "Have a good night, Rebecca."

Gathering my things, I start to walk up the stairs and I hear her following behind me.

She's really beginning to get on my nerves.

When I get outside, I spot Savannah walking toward the parking garage. I want to run after her, but I can still feel Rebecca's presence behind me.

"I'll see you on Wednesday, Luke," Rebecca says, appearing by my side. "Unless you want to grab a bite to eat right now. I'm starving."

When I look at her, she's pushing her chest out further like I'm all of a sudden gonna lose my mind over her. She's becoming more daring and blunter with her interest, I need to be a bit more direct with her since she's not getting it.

"Look, Rebecca. I think you're a beautiful woman," I start. "But I'm just not interested in that way."

Her eyes turn dark, almost angry as she lets out a cynical laugh, making my body shiver.

"I see," she says. "Well, I guess that's that. Goodnight, Luke."

I stand in place as I watch her walk away. I want to feel bad, but she is acting like I just betrayed her. I don't owe her anything, I can't force an attraction that's not there.

I shake my head in disbelief, then turn around and head toward the parking garage.

Savannah's car is gone but my phone beeps.

Savannah: Sorry, I didn't wait. I'm on my way back to your house.

It feels good knowing she's gonna be at my house when I get there. The end of this semester can't come soon enough.

I park my car next to hers in my garage, smiling.

I'm usually greeted by Vino when I open the door, but he's nowhere to be seen. I follow the commotion I hear coming from the family room. Savannah is on the floor laughing and playing with both dogs. She makes a sudden movement with her arms toward them, and they both run circles around her, then come back for more. Her laugh is uninhibited and infectious. I stand and watch in complete awe of the things she makes me feel.

Vino finally spots me and runs my way.

"Oh, hey," she smiles at me. "I already took them outside. We were just playin' around."

"I see that." I smile as I walk further into the room. "I think this is the first time I wasn't greeted by the door."

"Aw, are you jealous?" she jokes. "Do you not like that Vino loves me more now?"

I laugh. "Watch it, Princess."

"I was gonna make us some dinner. What're you in the mood for tonight?" she asks as she scrolls on her phone.

You. I think to myself. I'm only interested in eating her tonight.

"Whatever you want. I'm not picky," I say, tucking my thoughts away for now.

"Well, that's no help," she replies with a sigh. "Fine. I'll pick, but you can't complain about it if you're not in the mood."

"I'll complain if I want to," I say, walking into the kitchen with her.

I reach for a bottle of wine and pull out two glasses, handing her one.

"Cheers." I clink my glass on hers.

She takes a sip then starts rummaging through the fridge. She's wearing cutoff jean shorts. My dick stirs as I get a glimpse of the bottoms of her ass cheeks.

I wish I could pull them off and drag my tongue up her crack. I'm suddenly aware that I never got a chance to play with her ass. I hear her muffled, distant voice, but my brain is too distracted conjuring up images of my tongue and her ass.

"Luke!" I hear her shout through my fog.

I shake my head. "What?"

"Were you just staring at my ass?" she asks with her hip resting on the counter and a knife in one hand.

My eyes open wide. "Umm, I'll answer when you put the knife down."

She rolls her eyes and turns toward the counter and begins to cut some vegetables.

"Seriously, you're not making it easy to remain friends," she mumbles to herself.

"Excuse me." I lean forward, elbows resting on the counter. "You're the one who's strutting around here in shorts that show your ass cheeks when you bend over."

"Are you saying I'm dressing like a slut or something?"

My head falls back. Dammit. I didn't expect that to backfire.

She starts laughing then winks. "Kidding!"

I take another sip of wine and watch her as she throws olive oil and seasoning on the vegetables and puts them in the oven with some chicken.

She hops up on the counter and grabs her glass. We're now eye to eye. I look down at her legs and my eyes continue up to her face.

"How was your day?" she asks, oblivious to what she does to me.

I sigh. "It was alright. It's hard to get right back into the thick of it after a trip. There's a ton of paperwork that needs to be done for a new deal. But I did get a chance to speak to Giorgio on the phone a bit more as the contract is being written up. He told me to say hi."

A small blush forms on her cheeks.

"He's so sweet. I can't believe he even thought about me."

She underestimates the affect she has on people. She could change the world if she wanted to.

Without thinking, my hand comes up to her leg and runs up and down the length of it.

"Nobody could forget someone like you. You're too special."

She looks down at my hand then back up at me. Her hand reaches down to mine. Just as I think she's going to push it away, she gives it a squeeze.

"You make me feel different. Like I'm worth..." she struggles to get her words out. I see her trying to blink away tears then she shakes her head. "I don't understand what you see."

My head falls to the side as I study her for a second. "I know what I see. You just won't let yourself see it too. I'm not sure what is stopping you, but I'm going to change your mind one day. One day, you're going to look at yourself in the mirror and know your worth."

A tear escapes and runs down her cheek. I gently swipe it away with my thumb.

"Thank you," she whispers.

"No problem," I reply. "I'll catch all of your tears."

She shakes her head. "No, thank you for your words," she pauses, "and for catching my tears."

The timer beeps, pulling us out of the moment.

She jumps off the counter and takes the food out of the oven.

The mood has lifted as we eat at the table together. We quiz each other, each taking turns asking whatever question we want.

"Okay, I've got one." She giggles. Her second glass of wine clearly starting to get to her. "Tell me about you losing your virginity."

I groan. "Ask another question."

"What?" She throws her arm in the air, wine spilling over the rim. "Oops," she says as she wipes it off the table. "No! You have to answer."

"Fine," I concede. "I was sixteen. I was a sophomore, she was a senior. When I made the varsity baseball team, I became a starter which is a big deal as a sophomore. It put me on the map with the girls. I was at a party one night, and this beautiful senior, Kristy, came onto me. I guess she had assumed I was more experienced. She brought me upstairs and one thing led to another. I didn't know what the hell I was doing. I fumbled through the entire thing and ended up busting too soon and she was clearly disappointed in my performance. We haven't talked since."

She's resting her chin on her hand, covering her mouth so I can't quite see her reaction. "I'm sorry. That's horrible," she mumbles through her fingers.

"What?" I ask.

I pull her hand away and she's smiling.

"Are you trying not to laugh at my story?"

She scrunches her nose. "I'm sorry."

"I'll have you know, that was a pretty traumatic moment in my life."

"Oh, please. Based on our time together in Italy, I'd say you're over it. You're clearly an expert in bed now."

My eyes raise in interest. "Expert you say?"

"Let's not pretend that you don't know what you did to my body."

"I'd still like to hear you say it."

"I just did," she suggests.

"True."

We clean up our dishes and take the dogs out. As we walk back inside, she turns to me.

"Wanna watch a movie or something?"

"Sure. What do you want to watch?" I ask as I head to the couch and flop down.

"Hm." She thinks about it for a second. "Final Destination? Titanic?"

I throw my head back in laughter. "I've actually never watched Titanic," I admit.

She gasps in horror. "WHAT? You've *never* watched Titanic?"

I shrug my shoulders. "I guess I was too busy trying to get girls."

"Put that damn movie on now." She points to the TV. "Everyone has to see Titanic at least once in their lifetime."

"Isn't that movie like three hours?" I ask.

She nods her head but raises her eyebrows at me waiting for me to get on with it. I realize I'm not gonna win this battle.

The movie starts to play, and I realize we're both on opposite sides of the couch with Vino and Bailey snuggled between us.

It's oddly domestic and somehow feels so right.

I surprisingly don't hate the movie, which I don't admit at any point, and find myself lost in it throughout the entire night. It's close to midnight when it ends.

I stretch my arms over my head and yawn, surprised I made it to the end. Honestly, I should have already been in bed.

"I'm gonna regret staying up this late in the morning," I tell Savannah.

When she doesn't respond, I look over. Her head is lying on the armrest, and she's completely knocked out.

I take the time to look at her, her breathing slow and even. Everything in me wants to carry her to my bed, but I need to remember what this five-week arrangement is—and what it isn't.

Instead, I grab a blanket from a basket by the couch and lay it over her.

After letting the dogs out, I walk to my bedroom off a hallway from the family room. Vino follows behind and Bailey joins her mom on the couch.

The second our semester is over and final grades are in, I'm going to kiss Savannah like my damn life depends on it.

Chapter Twenty-Three

Savannah

I start to walk out of class, knowing there's no use trying to hang around, Rebecca will be glomming on to Luke. I haven't said anything to him about her, but the further we get into the semester, the more uneasy she makes me. I'm sure it's just jealousy. She's beautiful, and any moron can see she's interested in Luke.

Just as I'm getting to my car, I hear someone call my name.

I turn around and see Luke jogging up to me.

"How did you get out so fast?" I ask.

He shrugs. "I told Rebecca I wasn't interested in her the other day. I think she finally got the idea."

"You did?"

My heart flutters knowing he's pushing away beautiful women. Is it because of me?

He laughs lightly as he steps closer.

"Why do you look so surprised?" he asks as his fingers graze my cheek. "You know you're all I want."

Shit. I think I need medical attention. Is it normal for your heart to beat out of normal rhythm like this?

Despite possibly dying, I smile.

"Can I cook you dinner tonight?" he asks.

I nod my head, finding it hard to form any coherent words.

As he walks away, I get this odd feeling that someone is watching us. I look around the entire parking garage, and it appears that we were alone.

I'm all kinds of messed up right now. He's just so...dreamy. This semester can't end soon enough.

I'm so damn happy it's Friday. I just want to be lazy this weekend and hang around the house with Luke and the dogs.

You'd think nothing could compare to Italy and my time spent with Luke. Turns out it doesn't matter where we are or what we're doing; it's him and I that create the magic. I've never felt happier.

Luke shouldn't be far behind me. Class is out, and we drove separately but left at the same time.

I hear the garage door start to open and the dogs get excited and run to the door.

The three of us wait, knowing that our favorite person is about to walk through.

It opens, and he looks down at the dogs and back up at me then starts to chuckle.

"Hi, guys." He gives them both a pat.

He walks over to me and opens his arms, inviting me in for a hug.

Even though we can't be sexual, it doesn't mean we can't be affectionate. He's hugged me every day this week.

"And hi to you," he says as his arms engulf me.

"Hi." I sigh into his chest.

"I missed you today."

I look up at him. "You did?"

He smiles. "I did. It was a stressful day at work. I kept thinking all I needed to do was push through so I could see you."

I've never been in love before, but I think I love this man. There's just no way it gets better than this. We get lost in each other's eyes, neither one of us moving, and a loud knock at the front door makes me jump.

I'm holding the dogs back as Luke opens the door. I almost fall over with shock when I see who's standing there.

"Dad," I whisper.

Luke's eyes open wide as he looks between me and my father.

My father stands there, hands in his pockets, looking angrier than I've ever seen him.

"I assume you're Luke Giannelli," he says as he stares Luke down.

"I am, sir," Luke responds as he holds the door open. "Please, come in."

"How do you know?" I ask.

"Never mind how I know, Savannah," he snaps back.

My father steps in and we all stand in silence as the door is shut, awkwardness filling the room. My eyes already start to tear up as the two most important men in my life are right in front of me, but it's not like I had imagined. It's hard to admit I had already pictured what a future with Luke would look like. One where I introduce him to my father, they shake hands, and he proudly thanks Luke for loving his daughter.

Instead, my father is glaring at him like Luke is a monster.

My father seems to dismiss speaking any words to Luke and turns to me. "Go pack your things, Savannah."

"What? Dad, don't you want to talk about this?"

"Absolutely. You and I will talk about this at your apartment."

What apartment? "Dad, I already told my landlord I moved out."

"Not there. We're going to discuss you lying to me and moving out of the place you shared with the girls. I called Shannon's father. He told me your room is still open, the girls didn't find anyone to take it over. You're finishing out the semester there with your college friends."

I look over at Luke, expecting him to tell my father I can stay here, but he just stands there frozen. I see pure panic in his eyes as he looks at me.

"Dad. I'm staying here."

My father's head snaps toward me. "Savannah. You're not living with your professor. Now, please go pack your things. We can do this the easy way or the hard way."

"What?" I ask confused.

"If you come with me, I won't turn this man into the university. If not, my hands will be tied."

I gasp in shock. Who is this man? Why is he acting like this?

When I look at Luke, his face is white.

"Mr. Davis," Luke begins, but my father cuts him off.

"I'm not here to talk to you. This is between me and my daughter. You've done enough. Savannah, go pack. Now!"

Luke looks at me and nods his head.

"Go ahead, Savannah," he tells me.

Tears begin to cascade down my cheeks, but I know I can't put Luke in a bad spot, so I turn around and run upstairs.

I pack my bags through a steady stream of tears. Bailey sits by my side, a look of concern on her face, and Luke appears in the doorway.

"I'm gonna help you bring your things down," he whispers as he grabs a few bags.

"Luke," I cry.

He turns around to look at me. "I know, Princess," he says before walking down the stairs.

What else is there to say? We're stuck in an impossible situation.

Luke helps me load up my car, Bailey jumps into the backseat. She has no idea that she may never see Vino again. Just the thought of it brings a fresh new wave of tears. I can tell Luke wants to do something but doesn't know what.

He looks over at my father who's waiting by his car then back at me.

"Call me when you're settled back in," he whispers for only us to hear.

I nod my head and get in my car.

Dad told me to drive straight to the girls' apartment. We park and walk in silence up to the door.

It hits me that I don't have a key.

"I don't know if they're home, but I don't have a key anymore."

"They left it under the mat," he tells me. "I'm guessing you're going to have some explaining to do with them too. The way it sounded, your friends didn't know about any of this."

This is such a mess.

Luckily the apartment comes furnished, and once my dad gets me settled back into my room, we walk out to the main area and take a seat on the couch. I was hoping he was gonna head home afterward, but clearly, that isn't happening.

He sits in silence for a few minutes before speaking.

"How could you lie to me?" His eyes show pain and bewilderment. "I don't understand it—any of it. You lying about being able to afford your place, lying about where you live, about sleeping with your professor. That's not the girl I know."

"I'm sorry," I cry. "I know I've made a lot of bad choices these last couple months. I should've told you I couldn't afford this rent on my own, but I didn't want to stress you out. I know you're doing the best you can, and I just want you to be happy. You have Veronica and the kids to worry about now, and I don't want to be a burden."

"Dammit, Savannah. Why would you think you're a burden? You're my baby girl." He starts to choke up. "It's been you and me since your momma passed. Do you think I would ever be able to live in a world where you are unsafe? You're always my priority."

I shake my head repeatedly, trying to stop the tears from falling.

"It wasn't about being a burden. I just didn't want to see you struggle or stress about me. I wanted you to enjoy your life, without feeling like you had to help me out."

"My new life includes you, it in no way means you step *back* for others to come in, it means you step *aside*. There's a big difference. Do you understand that?"

I nod my head as tears continue to trickle down. "I'm sorry."

"I appreciate you loving me that much," he chokes up again, "to want me to be happy. But I'm not happy without you."

"Ok," my voice breaks.

"Was this professor a way of rebellion or something? Maybe you felt alone and were looking for someone to pay attention to you?" he asks, trying to understand.

I'm suddenly shocked and horrified. Is that what he thinks or me? That I would sleep with my professor for attention? The tears instantly stop.

"What are you saying, Dad?" I demand.

"It's just...not like you to do something like this," he struggles to get the words out. "I don't mean to offend you, sweetheart. I'm just trying to understand."

I try to calm down before I respond. I don't want the anger that's still coursing through me to make me say something I will regret. The three words that I haven't admitted to myself yet come to mind, and I blurt them out without even thinking.

"I love him," I cry. "Luke and me—we're so much more than what you're making us out to be. I've never met anyone like him. And it's killing me to hear you talk about us like we're some dirty little secret...like we need to be ashamed of what we feel."

He sighs. I get the feeling he doesn't believe me.

"Just give it some time. Focus on yourself and finishing school without anything getting in the way."

I don't like his response. It feels like he's completely discrediting my feelings.

"I'm not asking you to forget him right now. I'm just asking you to take a step back. It sounds like this all happened so fast, and at a pretty inappropriate time. No matter your feelings, you both know it's wrong. Do you understand what I'm saying?"

I nod my head. I'm too tired to fight right now.

"Good. I have to head home for work tomorrow. I wish I could hang around." He looks at me with concern. "You going to be alright if I go?"

Of course not, but I need him out of here. For the first time in my life, I'm struggling to even look at my father.

"I'm fine."

He sighs. "I'll call you tomorrow. One day, you'll see that this needed to happen. I love you, sweetpea."

Of course, he would use that nickname.

He gets up and walks out the door, leaving me alone to fall over in tears. I don't even know what any of this means. Luke and I were already doing what we needed to do. We haven't even kissed since we've been back.

Is my father ever going to look at Luke and see the man that he truly is?

From the couch, I can see the front door open, and the girls walk in laughing.

The moment they notice me, they drop everything and rush over. Aubrey and Shannon sit on my left and right, and Tricia sits on the floor by my feet. I'm surrounded by their love, but all I feel is shame. I don't deserve this; I lied to them and pushed them away.

"It's okay, Savi," Tricia says from the ground as her hand rubs my knee. "We're here."

"I'm—so—sorry," I cry out, my words getting lost through the tears.

Aubrey starts to rub my back. "No need to apologize."

They sit with me while I get out all the emotions that are pumping through me. After some time, the cries slow down before coming to an end.

I feel completely drained, so I lay my head back against the back of the couch. The girls sink into the couch as well, resting with me. Tricia leans her head down on my legs.

"Whenever you're ready to talk, we're here to listen," Shannon says.

"I don't even know where to start," I admit.

Silence falls among the four of us. I don't even know what exactly they are aware of.

"Let's start with why you didn't tell us you moved to one of the worst streets in the city instead of just telling us you needed help," Tricia says. "We could have each paid a little more rent. Anything to make sure you were safe and still with us. We were crushed to have you gone for the last part of our senior year."

I see tears start to form in her eyes. I had no idea it hurt them. I was so worried about inconveniencing them, that I didn't even *think* about hurting them.

"I didn't want to be a burden for you guys," I whisper, feeling the pain of admitting those words out loud.

"What?" Shannon gasps. "Burden us? You could *never* make us feel like that. We love you. It's not a burden to help the people you love."

"But I lied to you guys. I've pushed you away. How could you still want me around? Aren't you angry?"

"You did it with good intentions. With me, intention matters, and you didn't do it to hurt anyone. If anything, you did it because you thought you were doing us a favor," Aubrey tells me, which oddly makes me feel a bit better.

"Okay, can we move on to the good stuff? Like how you were living with our hot-as-sin professor without telling us? Please, please tell me you've seen his penis," Shannon says.

I laugh when I see that she is completely serious.

"Honestly, I think you need to see somebody," Tricia says to Shannon. "Like a sex addiction therapist or something."

Shannon rolls her eyes. "Oh, please, like you weren't sitting there wondering the same thing."

I look over at Aubrey who shrugs apologetically, letting me know Shannon may have a point.

Shannon is always the one in the group who says what others are thinking without a care in the world. As hard as it is to talk about, I tell them about Luke and me. From how it started, to where we are right now, also answering Shannon's brief questions like *how big is he* and *how good is he in bed?*

I get to the part where my dad suddenly appeared at Luke's front door, ready to drag me away like we were committing some massive crime and needed to be separated immediately.

"I just don't understand why he couldn't just call me first. Talk it out with me instead of barging in and taking over."

"He's your dad. He's worried about you. And he doesn't know Luke," Tricia says soothingly. "He's just trying to protect you. It's always been his job. Give him some time."

"I guess. I just wish he trusted me enough to know I wouldn't just sleep with a professor for a good grade or something like that. I...I love him."

Aubrey looks at me. "I don't want you to freak out on me. I'm only saying this because I love you. But don't you think your dad doesn't know what to think or if he can trust you when he finds out you've been lying to him all semester?"

I open my mouth to defend myself, but I can't think of anything to say.

She's right. Why would he trust me if I wasn't honest with him from the beginning? I lied about so much, he must think I've lost my mind. Maybe I have.

Shannon stands up. "I'm opening a bottle of wine, and we're going to binge some shows. A girl's night cures everything."

An hour into watching our favorite show, my phone buzzes in my pocket.

Professor Luke: How are you?

I don't know how to answer that question. Part of me is relieved to have everything out in the open and have my girls back, but I already miss Luke.

Me: Talked everything out with the girls. Luckily they don't hate me for lying. How are you doing?

Before he responds, I go into my contacts and change his name. We are well past him needing to be stored in my phone as Professor Luke. It's too impersonal.

Luke: Of course they don't hate you. They know your heart. I'm hanging in over here. Vino seems pretty depressed without her buddy. She's not the only one feeling that way.

I have to ask him.

Me: What are we supposed to do now?

I hold my breath as I wait for his response. I see the three little dots appear and disappear over and over. The suspense is killing me, and it's clear he's struggling with his words.

Luke: I don't know, Princess. Maybe we just need to give it some time. I don't want to come between your relationship with your father. That's too important and I wouldn't be able to live with myself.

Panic starts to restrict my breathing and my body starts to heat up.

Me: What're you saying?

This morning I woke up and was the happiest I had ever been. How did it all spiral so out of control?

Luke: Four more weeks in the semester. I don't want your dad finding out I haven't honored his request to stay away.

This feels like the first step in losing him. Four weeks will turn into him telling me it's never gonna work. Luke doesn't seem like the type of guy to go against a father's word. If my dad never comes around, I'll never be with Luke. A stabbing pain radiates in my chest at the thought of losing him.

Chapter Twenty-Four

Luke

One week without her. It's been impossible not to pick up the phone and call her. I walk into my house and am struck with such a strong feeling of loneliness.

I've never been lonely before, never felt like I needed a woman in my life. Once I caught a glimpse of what it's like to be with someone you truly care about, truly love...everything has changed.

The only reprieve I get are the ninety-minutes in class where I can see her from a distance. If that's all I can get, I'll take it.

When it's time to leave, she walks home with her friends, which makes me feel better. I'm glad she's safe and has her girls to be there for her.

I know she's disappointed that I told her we should keep our distance for now. I just hope she knows I am too. It's the last thing that I want.

But I also can't erase the look of pure disgust her father had for me.

I've been hell to be around at the office, that much I know.

I'm doing my best to read through a contract at my desk, when a knock at my door pulls me away.

"Come in," I shout.

Mia comes in with a file in her hand and a hesitant look in her eyes. A sign of the kind of grump I've been.

"Got the Mancini agreement right here. Thought you'd want the final look before we send it off for signatures."

"Thanks," I say as I lean across my desk to grab it.

I feel Mia staring at me, not making any move to walk out of my office.

"You need anything else?" I question her.

She takes a seat in front of me. "I thought you might need someone to talk to."

I lean back in my seat. "Why would you think that?"

She raises an eyebrow at me. "Come on. Let's not go through the part where you deny that something's wrong."

I sigh in defeat. "It's Savannah. A student of mine."

"The one living with you? The one from Gabe's wedding?"

How the hell does she know all of this?

"I take it Marcus told you," I say.

She shrugs like it's understandable. "He's worried. What about Savannah?"

"Her dad. He found out. Showed up at my door basically dragging her away."

"Oh, shit."

"Yeah."

"That's interesting."

"What's so *interesting* about it?" I ask.

"Well, I mean she's an adult. She can make her own decisions. Whether he agreed with them or not, I don't think he had the right to barge into your home and demand she leave."

I didn't expect that from Mia.

"It's still his daughter. He has a right to try and protect her. I'm just...I don't know. I'm struggling with the idea that anyone thinks they need to protect someone from me."

"I know. He just doesn't know you. Try not to take it personally. There are a lot of sick people in this world, so it's easy for someone to think the worst."

Her words slightly ease the guilt that has been clawing at me for the past week. They make me feel less like a monster and more...misunderstood, I guess. It's hard to put words to what I'm feeling.

"Thanks, Mia."

Hours later, I'm sitting on my couch. I poured a glass of wine from the Mancini farm. The smells and flavors bring me back to Italy.

Vino is lying next to me, her demeanor a bit somber compared to her usual excitement. She's been this way since Savannah and Bailey left.

Though only a week ago, it feels like forever since I was with Savannah. I miss her lips, her touch, her laugh, the way my heart would beat faster by something as simple as her eyes on me. Part of me regrets telling her we need to just take a step back until the semester is over. This would all be so much easier if I could hear her voice. I've wanted to pick up the phone and call her hundreds of times.

Every time I do, an image of her father comes to my mind. Then I think, if I ever have a shot at being with Savannah, I can't piss him off more.

I don't even know if I should go after her when she graduates. Family is important to me, it's everything. I've grown up with an amazing relationship with my parents and my siblings. I don't take it lightly that her father feels the need to protect his daughter from me.

I don't want to be any reason for their relationship to struggle.

Especially since it's been just the two of them for so long, they've shared a journey of such pain from the loss of her mother. Something like that must bond you together for life. I could never be the one to come in between them.

I'm afraid to ask her how they're doing. Have they talked more about the situation? Has she explained how we decided to keep it strictly platonic until after school? Would that even matter after what happened in Italy?

These questions keep scrambling around in my head, driving me absolutely insane.

I throw down the rest of the wine left in my glass and then walk into my bedroom. I unbutton my shirt and throw it in my dry-cleaning pile.

I need to go for a run. Maybe that will help me work off some of this access energy charging through me, creating a tidal wave of thoughts.

After I change, I pull out my running shoes. Vino eagerly wags her tail, knowing I never go on a run without her. I grab her leash and attach it to her collar.

"Come on, girl," I say to her. "Maybe we both need this run. I think we're both missing our girls tonight, aren't we?"

Chapter Twenty-Five

Savannah

Two more weeks left of school.

With each day that I don't have contact with Luke, I worry that he'll find being with me too difficult and walk away forever.

Going to class has been pure torture. Seeing him and knowing we can't talk, knowing I'm just another student. But this is what he thinks is right, and I get it, but my heart doesn't. It's all I can do to hold back my tears when I'm watching him in class.

Especially when I see Rebecca's appreciative eyes on him.

Just as class ends, I start to walk up the stairs with the girls. I turn around and see Rebecca look up at me with a sinister smile as she walks over to Luke's desk then sits on it.

Shannon looks back at me then at Rebecca. She instantly knows what I'm feeling.

"Come on," she wraps her arm around me. "Don't worry about her. She's clearly desperate. Have you seen the way she dresses for class? Any man with an ounce of class wouldn't be into her."

Her words give me enough confidence to not completely fall over in tears or run down those stairs and punch Rebecca in the face. Okay, I would never do that, but picturing it makes me feel a little bit better.

"What should we do on our second last Friday night as college students?" Tricia asks the group with excitement.

"There's a couple parties going on, we can go to a bar, or have a girl's night in," Aubrey suggests as we continue walking to our place.

I'm not really in the mood for anything but my bed. I know I need to go out with them and do anything in my power to soak up my time left. It's just so hard to do when it feels like you could be on the verge of losing someone you love.

"I vote for a party. Let's go out the way we came in. We used to always love going to parties," Shannon speaks up.

The rest of the girls agree. I nod my head that I'm in, afraid that if I speak, they'll hear the lack of enthusiasm in my voice.

Here I am, sitting on the deck of someone's house while music blares all around us. I'm sipping on my wine, realizing how far I've come in the four years that I've been here. I used to dance around with a beer in my hand as I flirted and laughed with people.

Now the music is loud, the people are annoying, and I want to be anywhere but here.

Shannon looks around the deck as other girls are stumbling and cracking up. "Is that what we used to be like? Why didn't anybody slap us in the face?"

I almost spit up the wine I'm drinking as a laugh escapes me.

"I'm so glad you said that. I thought I was the only one feeling that way," I admit.

"I refuse to believe that was us four years ago," Tricia says.

"Unfortunately, that was exactly what we looked like," Aubrey says with a cringe.

We all look back at the party. I don't think we realized how we've all changed until now. We came into this school as immature, brand new adults. Not a care in the world, just looking to have a good time. We're leaving with more real-world experience, hoping to find a path in life that makes us all happy.

I think I hear Tricia sigh. "I can't believe it's all over."

The reality of the moment hits us and silence falls upon our group.

Wherever we end up next, I just hope that we can still stay connected. I hate that I lost most of my last semester with them. All because I let pride get in the way, and though it's hard to admit, a part of me didn't think I was worth the trouble for anybody. I don't know where this insecure part of me came from, but Luke was able to show me how to love myself more. He showed me what I was doing to myself, how I was the one belittling myself. Once you see that, how do you not make steps to start and change it?

I don't want to be the reason that I'm unhappy.

"What do you say we go home, bake goodies, and drink more wine?" I suggest, just wanting more quality time with them.

They all turn around toward me. "Yes!" they agree in unison.

"Let's eat so much sugar that we need to switch to sweatpants," Shannon suggests. "That's how you know you did it right."

We walk back to our apartment and Shannon gets started on the cookies right away. The girl is serious about her desserts.

I open the bottle of wine and pour our glasses. We all huddle around the island, drinking while we watch Shannon.

"Let's play truth or dare," Aubrey suggests. The wine is starting to kick in and we're getting a bit loose and silly. Truth or dare sounds fun. "I'll start. Tricia, truth or dare," Aubrey asks.

Tricia bites her bottom lip as she considers her options. Your option all depends on who's asking.

"Truth."

"Hmm." Aubrey taps her finger on her chin as she thinks. "What's the kinkiest thing you've done since being at college?"

I throw my head back and laugh. Aubrey is such a good-ie-two-shoes. We mess with her all the time because she is so inexperienced and shy when it comes to sex. Even now, her cheeks are turning red at the idea of sharing this with us.

"Umm, ugh, you suck for this question," she says. "I mean I gave my first blowjob this year. That was kinky."

Shannon almost drops the tray of cookies on the way to the oven. "You had sex before you ever put your mouth on a guy's dick?"

Aubrey looks around at us. "Of course! That's so gross. I never wanted to."

"So, what did you think about it?" Aubrey asks.

"It wasn't as bad as I thought it was going to be," she admits. "I wasn't a huge fan of all the cum in my mouth."

The three of us start laughing hysterically at Tricia's admission.

"Ok, fine! My turn!" she shouts. "Shannon. Truth or dare."

Shannon leans against the island with a smile. "Truth. I don't want you pulling me away from these cookies. They're almost done."

"What's the kinkiest thing *you've* done," Tricia asks.

"Oh, gosh," Aubrey says. "I don't think I wanna know the answer to this."

Shannon gives her an evil eye. "I'm not that crazy. I don't know. Off the top of my head, I'd say...I let Austin lick my asshole."

"Ewww!" Tricia screams. "That's so gross!"

Shannon winks at her. "Don't knock it 'til you try it."

"So, you liked it?" Aubrey asks curiously.

"Yeah. It felt really good." Shannon looks over at me with a gleam in her eyes. "Savannah. Truth or dare."

Oh, God. She's gonna ask me the same damn question. I think back to Italy and everything Luke and I did. It feels oddly personal and something I don't want to share with anybody right now, not when I may burst out in tears at the thought of never experiencing it again. I look down at the remaining contents of wine in my glass and take the last gulp.

"Dare."

"Oooooh," the girls say together.

"I can't believe you chose dare," Aubrey says to me. "You do know that's Shannon, right?"

Shannon is looking at me with dazzling determination. Crap! Why did I choose dare with Shannon?

"I dare you," she starts "to video call Professor Hottie right now."

Another set of oooh's fall from the girls' lips.

"What? I can't. You know he said we should keep our distance until school is over."

"Yeah, but you also slept with the guy and are in love with him. It's not like you're showing up on his doorstep. Plus, you've been miserable with no contact."

I wish she wasn't so perceptive. She knows the distance has been killing me. But I can't call him, it seems so desperate. I don't want him to get mad at me.

"What happens if she won't do it?" Tricia asks. "I don't think any of us have ever backed down from a dare before."

Those words alone make me pick up the phone. I'm sure as hell not gonna make history as the first person to back down from a dare on our last night playing this game together. I scroll through my phone until I find his name and click on the video icon.

My heart is beating erratically as my uneasiness grows by the second. Before I can end the call and hide away in my room, his face appears on the screen.

His hair is all messed up like he's been pulling at it, and he appears to not have a shirt on, but his smile is bright.

"Hi," I say gently.

"Hi, Princess," his raspy voice responds.

The girls are making lovesick faces at his nickname for me. Aubrey's hand is over her heart like she can't take it. I look up at them and try to convey a message of shut up, but I'm caught by Luke.

"What's going on? What's that look for?" he asks curiously.

"Hi, Professor Luke," Shannon screams.

My head falls in my hand with embarrassment. I can't believe I couldn't go more than two seconds without being caught. An unwelcome blush creeps up on my cheeks.

"Hi, ladies," he answers. "I'm guessing I'm talking to your possie right now?"

I nod my head still feeling the sting of humiliation.

"Sorry," I tell him. "I just...wanted to say hi."

He smiles at me. "Never apologize for calling me."

Swoon. Can he be any sweeter? Even when he has annoying college girls laughing in the background, he seems patient and easy-going.

"I'm gonna go in my room for a second. Hang on," I tell him. I look at the girls. "I'll be back."

"Hurry back," Shannon says. "Cookies are done!"

I walk quickly to my bedroom, closing the door behind me. Bailey follows me and we both get on the bed.

"You enjoying your night?" he asks with his arm now resting behind his head.

Shit, his biceps are bulging from that position. He is so damn sexy, it's not even fair.

"I am," I smile. "We were trying to do something commemorative of our time together. We started at a house party like the old days." My mouth cringes at the thought of it. "We didn't realize how young and immature we were back then. I think we lasted about fifteen minutes before we decided to come back to our apartment and drink wine."

"And bake cookies," he adds with a smile.

I laugh. "And bake cookies."

"It doesn't sound much more mature than the house party, I know."

He laughs. "You know my brother, Marcus. He's years out of college and still hasn't grown up. I think a night in baking and drinking wine sounds exactly like what Gabe's wife Alexis would be into."

How does he do it? He takes my insecurities and makes me feel better. No matter what, he never seems to judge me.

"I miss you," I whisper as I turn to my side.

He looks at me through the phone like he really sees me. "Me too, Princess."

"I know you said no more contact."

"It's not easy. I get it. I've wanted to pick up my phone every second of the day for the last couple weeks."

I sigh in relief. He has no idea how much I needed to hear those words.

"Woman! Cookies are ready, let's go. It's ladies' night," Shannon shouts through the door.

I roll my eyes. "Sorry. I should go. It's supposed to be a girls' thing tonight."

He smiles. "Go. Enjoy this time. It goes by too quickly."

"Bye, Luke."

I open the door and Shannon is standing there with the biggest smile on her face.

"That man is crazy about you," she says.

We walk back to the kitchen together. I want to believe her, but my heart is still afraid to get it's hopes up.

"There's no way you can tell from that call," I reply.

Tricia laughs. "Girl. It is absolutely obvious that he's completely smitten with you. And holy crap, is he hot. I caught a glimpse of that shirtless man."

The beginning of a smile tips at the corners of my mouth. I hope that's true, because I'm so gone for this man.

Chapter Twenty-Six

Luke

"Are you okay, Uncle Luke?" Sienna, my niece, asks me.

We're sitting on the floor of my parents' home, my childhood home in Little Italy, playing war. It's been going on for ten minutes, each of us thinking we're about to win then losing an ace or a face card to the other person. I'm only half interested in the game, pretty much how I've felt for the last month.

It's like the world lost most of its color the day Savannah was forced out of my life.

I keep telling myself it was the right thing to do, but I can't deny that it's not at all what I wanted to do.

Is there a possibility that what's right isn't always black and white? That's normally how I've lived my life, no grey area. I'm the rule follower, and you either follow them or don't. This is the first time that everything in me has been desperately telling me to say *fuck it* to what looks right or what others tell me is right and do what makes me happy.

But there's the small problem with what the people in Savannah's life think is right, like her father.

I can't just barge back into her life and ruin her relationships.

I look down at my niece, who's patiently waiting for my response, surprised that she can see through my façade. Is it that obvious to everybody what I'm feeling on the inside?

"I'm good, Sisi girl," I tell her. "I'm just wondering which one of us is finally gonna come through and win this game."

She smiles. "It'll be me."

I chuckle. "Are you sure about that?"

"I have three of the four aces, I'm clearly gonna win."

She wasn't wrong. Five minutes later she takes my last card.

"Nice game," I tell her as we both stand.

"Dinners ready," Ma calls from the kitchen.

Everybody squeezes in around the table, covered in Ma's white tablecloth with a little lace at the end. It may be 2023, but you wouldn't know it if you walked into my parent's home. But I love it. It makes me think of my childhood, back before the world turned you into a cynical adult.

"Can I help you, Ma?" Gabe asks as she carries two heavy plates to the table.

He meets her halfway and grabs them out of her hands. It's a bit of odd behavior for Gabe, but I don't think too much of it.

"Looks incredible, my dear," Pa says as he's opening the bottles of wine sitting in the center of the table. With seven adults, we always need several bottles for dinner.

Pa goes around and begins to pour the wine. When he gets to Alexis, she smiles at him.

"I think I'll skip the wine tonight," she says.

Stunned silence falls upon the room. Alexis has never once refused a glass of wine. Before I can even get to the thought, Mia screams, "You're pregnant!"

Gabe groans. "I told you just let them pour the wine. You didn't have to drink it."

Well, that confirms it.

Ma and Mia are out of their chairs, hugging Alexis and Gabe, and Ma starts to cry.

I stand up myself and give Alexis a kiss on the cheek. "Congrats, sis," I say then I shake Gabe's hand.

Once we all get seated, Pa raises his glass of wine. "A toast," he begins, "to a new healthy baby boy or girl. Congratulations, Alexis and Gabe."

We all lift our glasses and salute.

The dinner is filled with conversation surrounding the news. Alexis and Gabe are smiling from ear to ear, constantly looking at each other and sneaking kisses.

For the first time ever, I'm jealous. I realize how much I want that.

Savannah's smiling face comes to mind as she rubs her growing belly.

Shit, now I'm thinking about her pregnant with my baby. You would think this would get easier, yet the more time away, the harder it gets.

"Hey, Luke," Mia calls from across the table. "Help me with the dishes."

I stand up and start taking everybody's empty plates then follow her into the kitchen. I start to rinse while she loads the dishwasher.

I wonder what Savannah's doing right now. Ever since she called me a week ago, I've been hoping it would become a routine. I want nothing more for her to break the rules and call me, since I have such a hard time being the rule breaker.

Instead, she's stuck to our agreement of distance, and the only time I've seen her is during class.

"Okay, I've given you enough time to navigate this yourself," Mia says, pulling me from my thoughts. "Clearly, you need a little bit of sisterly advice."

I sigh. "What do you mean?"

"You're not happy."

"How can you tell?" I hand her another plate.

"You don't smile anymore. If you do, it isn't real. You just go to work and go home."

I don't know what to say to that. Instead of speaking, I just focus on getting the task at hand complete.

"Have you talked to her?" she asks.

"She called me once last week. We basically said hi and that was it."

"What are you gonna do next week when the semester is over?"

"I want to call her. But there's this weird voice in the back of my head telling me that if it was wrong a week ago, it won't magically be right now."

"It's not wrong. You just can't be involved while she's your student. It's like if you were her boss, you couldn't date. But if she quit, it would be okay."

Hmm. When she says it like that, it doesn't feel wrong at all.

"I don't think her father would appreciate me contacting her," I admit.

She puts the last plate in the dishwasher, closes it, then leans on the counter.

"You know," she says, arms crossed over her chest, "what you did wasn't that bad. You're talking about it like she was a minor or something. I've already said my peace about what her father did."

Before I can reply, we're interrupted. Everybody starts walking into the kitchen holding the remainder of the plates and bowls. They clearly know something is going on by the abrupt pause in our conversation.

"What's wrong?" Ma asks.

I shrug like it's no big deal. "Nothing."

I can tell nobody believes me, but I have absolutely no interest in making this a family intervention.

"I think he's still upset that he got busted by his student's father for sleeping around with her," Marcus blurts out.

"Dude! What the fuck?" I bark back at him.

I can't believe he did that. I still haven't had the nerve to tell my parents what happened. I've been meaning to, but every time I start, the words get stuck in my throat.

"What?" Ma gasps in surprise. "When? With who?"

"It happened weeks ago," I say shamefully, eyes focused on the ground.

"It was the girl from the wedding," Marcus joins in. "Savannah."

Ma's face brightens. "She was a very sweet girl. Beautiful too."

She should be scolding me by now.

"He's been miserable since. I'm trying to convince him to call Savannah," Mia tells everybody.

"Why didn't you tell me?" she asks, hurt etched in her voice.

I look away from her, not wanting to see the pain in her eyes. "I didn't want you to be disappointed in me."

The words break as I try to make sure I don't cry. I hate crying in front of people, just about as much as I hate disappointing anybody.

"You think we'd be disappointed?" Ma asks.

I confirm with another head nod, still not looking at her. Next thing I know, I feel a slap on my arm.

"Ow!" I shout. "What the hell was that for, Ma?"

"You stupid boy! I don't care what mistakes you make—I'll always love you. Sure, you shouldn't have touched her while she was your student. But I know you, I know you must feel strongly for her. It's not like you to break a rule, so she must be somethin' special."

"I know you'll love me. I don't want to disappoint you."

She shakes her head. "You've always held yourself to impossible standards. You would cry if you got anything lower than a B+ in school cuz you thought we'd be mad."

Marcus laughs in the background. "Damn. I would've celebrated a B+."

"That's because you're a moron," Gabe smacks him then winks at me.

Marcus just laughs again and nods his head. He's used to the teasing, even though he knows we're kidding. He's a damn smart guy and an asset to our business.

Ma mumbles something in Italian under her breath.

"When is school over?" Pa asks.

"Next week," I answer.

"Are you gonna call her?" he continues.

"I don't know. Obviously I want to, but I'm afraid her dad will never be okay with us. I know if I go back to her, we're gonna be together. There's something big between us. I also know that I could never be the one who gets in between her and her father. She lost her mother when she was young, she can't lose what she has with her father."

"Huh," Pa says.

"What?" I ask him.

"Well, it seems to me that that's something between her and her father. If he chooses to throw a fit and not approve, he will only have himself to blame for a broken relationship. It won't be your fault. You're a good man, Lucas. Don't let anybody make you feel any differently."

"Thanks, Pa."

Alexis fans her face as tears start to stream down her cheeks. "Don't mind me. Pregnancy hormones."

It breaks the tension and makes me laugh.

"I'm gonna get going. I have a lot to think about. But thanks for being so supportive. It really means a lot," I tell them.

As I'm walking out the door, Ma grabs my face and gives me an unnecessary amount of kisses on my cheek.

I think about my dad's words as I drive home. Pa doesn't speak up often, but when he does, you listen. If he thinks that's true, that if her father won't approve, it would be on him, not me—that changes everything. The question is, do I think he's right? Can I get over what could happen to them and worry about what her and I want?

Chapter Twenty-Seven

Savannah

The light shines down in my eyes, forcing me to open them to the world. I do my best to ignore it and go back to sleep, but to no avail. When I open them again, I see Bailey standing by my bedroom door, wagging her tail. She's always been so patient. She won't wake me, even when she desperately needs to go to the bathroom.

But she'll make it very obvious when I'm awake that she would very much like to go outside.

I smile at her. "You wanna go outside?"

She scoots around excitedly, tail wagging at full speed.

I pull myself out of bed, not bothering to change out of my pajamas yet, and open the door.

Just as I'm about to open the front door, there's a knock. I open it cautiously, wondering who it could be at this hour.

"Hi, honey" Veronica, my stepmom, says with a smile.

I'm shocked to see her standing here alone.

"Hi..." I stare at her.

"I know this is a surprise. I was hoping I could take you out to breakfast before your first class."

I know she's been a little lonely lately. My stepsiblings Lainey and Gavin are with their father for the month of May. I wonder if this has anything to do with that.

"Umm, yeah, sure," I reply with a smile, not wanting to be rude, but still a bit skeptical about her visit.

I wonder if my dad sent her. I've been texting with him to let him know I'm okay, but I'm still just struggling to move on like nothing happened.

A big smile instantly takes up her face. "Great."

"Of course. Come on in, I just need to get ready. I'm gonna let Bailey out first, I'll be right back."

An hour later, we're sitting outside on a beautiful patio covered in flowers. We picked a table in the shade, so we didn't die from the heat, which is starting to become unbearable these days. The humidity in Ohio can sneak up on you.

"How are you doing?" she asks me after she taking a sip of her coffee.

"I'm doing pretty good." It's my typical response to the question whenever anybody asks these days.

What else can I say? That I lie awake at night, missing him so much it hurts. Nobody wants to hear that.

She sighs. "Maybe you can answer again but be honest this time. I'm here for you, to see how you're doing. I'm not here for your father."

I'm a little taken aback by her response. It's more forward than she's ever been with me. She appears genuine, not being judgmental or threatening.

"I'm...sad. I miss him. It's been really hard to be in class and pretend like we don't know each other. It's hard to think back to how humiliating it was to have Dad storm into his house and demand I leave like I was a child."

She cringes. "I told him not to do it. He was so worried you were being taken advantage of, that this was some professor who does this to all of his students, that he couldn't see reason."

"Luke is nothing like that. Even if he was, it would've been my decision. But I would like to think that my own father knows me better than that. I'm not that the type of person. Luke isn't a full-time professor. He volunteered for one semester unpaid while the university finds a permanent replacement. So, no, Luke doesn't make a habit of this."

Her shoulders seem to drop in relief, letting go of her uncertainty.

"I'm happy to hear that. So, you two aren't talking right now?"

"No. We weren't even doing anything with each other when Dad stormed in. We made an agreement to wait until after the semester. Now that Dad scared the crap out of Luke, he said we shouldn't have *any* contact until the semester is over."

Veronica smiles. "He sounds like a good man."

"He is."

"Your father misses you," she says with sadness etched in her voice.

"I just need some time. Does he see how wrong his actions were?" I ask.

She seems to ponder my question. "Yes and no. He still is so protective of you. He's so angry with you and himself that you didn't tell him you needed help financially. I know you've had more heartache in your life than most people have to endure, but I think it made you go into some kind of survival mode. You walk around like you don't want to burden the world, when you need to open up to the love the world can offer you."

Her words hit so much, tears threaten to surface.

I do close myself off to the world when things get difficult. I guess it's the only coping technique I have. Dad did the best he could, but he was grieving his own loss when my mother passed. I had to learn how to deal with things on my own.

"I know. I could've lost a lot of amazing people in my life simply because I was too scared to open myself up and be vulnerable. This whole thing has definitely been a huge eye-opener for me. But I do need him to see how he handled it was wrong. He pushed away the most important person in my life."

"You love him." A statement, not a question.

I shake my head as a single tear falls down my cheek. I wipe it quickly so nobody around us can see.

"I do," I whisper, then pull my sunglasses down to cover the embarrassment I feel.

She smiles. "I can tell."

"How?" I ask curiously.

"Well, a woman knows when another woman is hurting over a man. I can tell from the brief time we've spent together that you're different now. I would say a bit sadder on the surface, but also, there's something else. Meeting him has changed you. You seem more grounded in life."

I'm surprised by her words. I do feel different now, like meeting him put a different perspective on life. He opened my eyes to what love is. I'm a changed person.

"I'm gonna work on your father. He'll get there, just give it some time. But your graduation is coming up next week. I do think you should put this aside temporarily so you two can enjoy the moment together. You don't want to look back and feel like there was a rift between you guys during a huge moment in your life."

She's right. He's the reason I'm here today, getting ready to accept my diploma. He never let my mother's sudden death steal any love from my life.

"I'll call him," I tell her.

She smiles. "Good. And it doesn't mean you have to forgive him right now, it just means you put it aside for right now."

I nod my head in agreement.

"Thank you for driving all the way up here for me."

"Of course, honey. You're my family now, too. I know we don't know each other that well yet, but I do look forward to growing our relationship."

Her words make my eyes water with such emotion. Can it be that at the age of twenty-two, I finally have a mother figure in my life? It's something I've desperately wanted all my life. I used to pray for it every night in bed when I was younger.

We spend the rest of breakfast just getting to know each other and enjoying our time together. I didn't realize how much I just needed some kind of unconditional love and support until now.

She's made me feel heard and it's such a gift. I feel stronger and more confident in my own life decisions.

This is my life to live, and for once, I'm not going to apologize to anybody for it.

We hug each other with the promise to see each other next week for my graduation. I also promise to give my dad a call on the way to my first class.

I pull out my phone as soon as I get into my car. With one last reminder that I'm strong and know what's right in my life, I click on his name.

"Savannah," he answers, sounding surprised. "I'm so happy to hear from you."

"Hi, Dad."

"How are you doing?" he asks.

"I'm good. Just had breakfast with Veronica, although I'm sure you're aware of that."

He sighs. "I was worried when she said she was going up to talk to you. I hope she didn't overstep any boundaries."

"No, it was really nice talking to her."

An awkward silence falls upon us, something that has never happened before.

"I just wanted to call to tell you that I'm looking forward to having you and Veronica at my graduation next week. I'm still struggling with what you did to Luke, I'm not sure exactly what it will take for me to move past this, but I do want to celebrate my day with you."

It sounds like he's sniffling in the background, like he's crying.

"I never wanted to hurt you. I just wanted to protect you," he whispers.

"I don't need protecting anymore. I'm an adult now. If you have something to say, or a question on how I'm living my life, you can talk to me about it. You can't storm in and take over." I don't know where the courage to say these words is coming from, but I keep going, "Now, I know I messed up with the lies. I will own that part. I have some things that I need to work on, one is being open and honest with people despite what they will think. This is my first step in that direction. I'm telling you, that even if I made a mistake, which I'm sorry for, you made one too."

"I don't know what you want me to say," he says.

"I don't know either. Maybe a sorry—an acknowledgment that what you did was wrong."

Silence.

I don't understand what's so hard about just admitting he was wrong. This feels like a side of him I've never dealt with before.

"You know, just forget it, I'm clearly asking for too much. I'll see you next week. Bye, Dad," I say and hang up.

I'm so fuming mad. It's hard to picture even going to class today. Thank God I have two more days of school left. Although, that means today is Thursday, and I don't have class with Luke. A part of me could really use being in the same room with him.

Chapter Twenty-Eight

Luke

"Can you believe it's the last day of class?" Rebecca asks me as we stand up front, waiting for the students to roll in.

"Nope. It's definitely flown by," I say as I continue to look down at the paper in my hand.

I'm doing anything I can to avoid talking to her. This is thankfully the last time we will see each other. She still doesn't seem to get the idea that I'm not interested. I've given up and now just do my best to avoid it.

The students start to walk in, and my eyes are trained on the door, waiting for her.

This is it. Our last day of this bullshit before we can move on for good. I barely got any sleep last night, I was so excited for this day to come.

I spot her friends before her, but when I see her, my breath gets caught in my lungs. She's in a white flowy dress that makes her look more gorgeous than ever. I'm still shocked she can garner such a reaction from me even after five months.

She and her friends are laughing as they walk down the stairs and take their seats in the front.

I don't even care anymore what people think of me, I'm too struck by her beauty to look away. When she spots me, she smiles.

I find myself smirking at her. I think she dressed up for me today and that makes me feel so damn good.

There's a certain energy in the air, the last day of school. I don't know if it's just me or if everyone in this room is feeling it. This class is just a wrap-up of the entire semester, and a time for everyone to ask any exit questions.

To my surprise, the questions the students ask are thoughtful and engaging. It completely distracts me from what today means. I find myself enthusiastically answering their queries. With each stolen glance her way, my body gets more excited for the time to be up. Although, today isn't going to be exactly what I want it to be, I can at least talk more honestly with her. I don't have to hold back.

By the end of the ninety-minutes, I'm surprised it went by as quickly as it did.

"Well, that's all the time we have folks. I want to thank you for making my semester here so special. I had an excellent time and hope you all took something from this class. You have my email on the syllabus if you ever want to reach out with any further questions."

And that's a wrap. Everyone packs up their things. There's hoots and hollers, this being the last class for everybody on a Friday evening. For some, it's their last class ever. For others, they'll be back after summer.

I see Rebecca ready to make a beeline for me, so I grab my bag and make quick work to join the students as we exit the auditorium.

I wait by the stairs outside of the building, hoping to steal a moment with her.

I'm leaning on the bottom railing when she appears at the door with her friends. Her eyes are frantically scanning her surroundings, a slightly panicked look on her sweet face. When she spots me, I smile.

Her face turns from panic to joy in a matter of seconds. I love that I can do that to her. It's the single greatest feeling that I've ever experienced.

When she approaches, her friends give her a small wave as they walk away. Shannon, I think her name is, winks at me.

I small laugh escapes. She's definitely a character, but I like her. She seems like a good friend to Savannah.

Savannah stands on the step just above me so we are equal height. It gives me the chance to look into her green eyes. I could get lost in them for hours, but right now I need to talk to her.

"Hi," she whispers.

"Hi, Princess."

She smiles, bites her lip, and looks down at the ground bashfully. I want to grab her and kiss her lips that I've longed for since the moment they lost connection in Italy. But first, there are some loose ends I want to tie up before we go down that road.

"You look beautiful," I tell her. "Were you thinking of me when you dressed for class?"

She nods her head and I have to suppress the growl of satisfaction that wants to escape.

"So, listen, I wanted to tell you that I've been looking forward to this day for weeks."

"Me too," she admits.

"But there is something I need to do before we can be together. I just need to know one thing," I start. She looks at me confused and slightly saddened. "Do you trust me?"

"Of course."

Relief floods my body. I was worried she wouldn't give me the answer I was looking for.

"Good. Can you give me some time to come up with a game plan and trust that I'll be back for you?"

As much as the look of disappointment in her eyes kills me, I know that in order for me to move forward, it has to be this way. It's the only way I know I can be present with her one hundred percent without any reservations. She deserves that, and I want to be able to give her everything she deserves.

"Umm," she hesitates. "Yes, I can do that. It's not gonna be like a year or something, right?"

I laugh. "I couldn't last an entire year without you in my life."

Her cheeks blush at my words. But it's true. I can't imagine a year without her. Since we met, she's become the first thing on my mind in the morning, and the last thing I think about before I fall asleep. She has become the motivation in my life. It's all about when I get to see her next, when I get to touch her.

"Okay," she says on an exhale. "I trust you."

"Good," I smile.

I start to back away, but when I take one last glance at her, I can't hold back. I take two big steps back toward her, grab her cheeks, and slam my mouth down on hers. I swallow down her gasp. I can't stop, I won't. This is everything that I've needed.

My body starts to feel whole again as my lips devour hers with my mercy. I don't even care who the hell is around us, who sees it, because this is no longer something we have to hide. Fuck anyone who tells me she isn't mine. She's been mine since the moment I laid eyes on her.

Her tongue shyly mixes with mine, and I groan into her mouth. Fuck, she's gonna kill me. I just want to take her right here, right now. But that, unfortunately, is wrong.

When it becomes clear it's either fuck her in front of the entire campus or pull away, I put my hand on her hips and push myself off her.

We're both breathing like we just ran a damn marathon.

"I thought you needed time first," she starts, but I put my finger to her lips to stop her.

"I'm a weak man when it comes to you," I smile. "That was one kiss to remind you what we have."

"Like I could forget."

I laugh as I start to back away. "That's what I like to hear, Princess. I'll see you soon."

She nods her head, and I turn around and walk away.

Okay, so that didn't go exactly to plan. I hadn't planned on fucking her mouth with my tongue, but it was a welcomed improvise. I don't regret it. I think she needed that to know I wasn't bluffing, that I'd be back for her, and soon.

But first, I have to figure something out. I need a plan, and I need one now.

Chapter Twenty-Nine

Savannah

"Holy shit. It's here guys. Can you believe we're graduating?" Shannon shouts from the kitchen.

I'm in my bathroom curling my hair in my black dress and heels. It does feel strange that the day is finally here. Four years of my life seem to have gone by in the blink of an eye. It feels like just yesterday I was moving into my dorm room, meeting Shannon for the first time as my roommate. She was a force to be reckoned with, and I won't lie, she scared the shit out of me at first.

Now we're all here, about to say goodbye to this chapter of our lives.

My phone, sitting on the countertop, beeps with a message.

I glance down.

Luke: Good luck today, Princess. We'll see each other soon.

Okay, I know I trust him, but COME ON!! What the hell does he need to do in order for us to move forward? He's not going to continue teaching at the university, so it's not like he will need to inform them that we're gonna start seeing each other. I can't, for the life of me, think of what it is.

It does feel good that he is at least reaching out. It's been six days since he knocked me off my feet with his kiss. I didn't see it coming, but it was easily the best kiss of my life. I can't see a kiss being more perfect than that.

That panty-melting, toe-curling kind of kiss that has so much emotion and longing behind it.

I'm not ashamed to admit I needed to take care of myself that night when I lay awake letting the memory wash over me.

"Time to go," Aubrey says from the other room. "Come on, ladies. We can't be late. Our parents are waiting for us outside of the gym."

Graduation is being held in our basketball gymnasium. It's going to be a hot and sweaty couple hours while they call each and every name of the graduating class.

I look in the mirror to make sure I look good enough for the many pictures that will be taken today. I unplug the curling iron, turn the light off, and grab my phone.

"Okay, I'm all set," I say as I join the girls by the front door.

"We need a selfie before all the commotion begins," Tricia says. She holds her phone out as we all squeeze into the frame.

Once the picture is taken, we pile into Shannon's car. None of us have any interest in walking in our heels, so we opted to pay the ridiculous parking costs for a prime spot. This gives me just enough time to pull my phone out.

Me: Now isn't soon enough.

Does that sound too desperate? I don't care, it's the truth.

His response is almost immediate.

Luke: <3

Ugh, cryptic much? My patience is waning. Instead of replying, we're already parked and ready to go.

When we get to the front of the building, it's filled with hundreds of students and even more family and friends. Our parents said they would meet us here before we go in. They want some pictures before the ceremony.

"There they are," Aubrey says as she spots them leaning against the brick wall.

I find my dad and Veronica and lean in for a hug.

"Hi, Dad," I say as he wraps his arms around me.

"Sweetpea. I'm so damn proud of you," he says then looks away and coughs.

Veronica hugs me next. "Good grief, Mitch. I told you we should've packed tissues. You're already tearing up."

I laugh. "Is it that shocking that I earned a bachelor's degree?"

"No, of course I knew you could do it. It's just scary how fast it all came and went. You're no longer my little girl."

Veronica smiles at us.

"I haven't been little for quite a while," I point out.

Before he has the chance to answer, the students are being told to get inside and in our places.

The girls and I wave to our parents and start toward the door. The folding chairs are lined up in neat rows all over the gymnasium floor for the graduating students. Thankfully, they got rid of any attempts at assigned seating. Me and the girls snatch some seats on the end of a row in the middle of the gym floor.

It takes another thirty-minutes before they get all the guests inside and seated in the bleachers.

Although, with Shannon sitting with us, thirty-minutes doesn't lack entertainment. She started playing a game called 'Find the Guys We've Hooked Up With.' We're didn't exactly sleep around, so it was very underwhelming.

She found two guys between the four of us.

"Okay, so it's not that many," Shannon says in her defense.

"That's because you somehow forgot we aren't whores who went around sleeping with so many guys that we could make a game out of it," Aubrey says.

I chuckle at Shannon's reaction.

"Welcome students, family, and friends," the dean begins.

Silence falls upon the room. For the next several hours, we all try to stay awake while they go A-Z throughout the graduating class. I was lucky enough to get it over with rather quickly having the last name Davis.

"And the final graduate of the class of 2023," I hear said in the background.

Thank God! It's over!

"Congratulations, class of twenty twenty-three."

Hoots and hollers erupt as we all stand up and celebrate.

People begin trying to run out of the gym, a true sign that these things take way too damn long.

I follow the girls outside to a spot along the wall where we agreed to meet our parents. The summer sun is shining down on my black cap and gown, not the most comfortable combination.

"Anyone else sweating balls under here?" Tricia asks as she fans herself with the program.

"Why black?" Aubrey asks.

"There they are," Aubrey's mom shouts enthusiastically.

Once all our parents are here, we take more photos. Some with parents and daughter, and a bunch of the four of us girls.

I'm leaning against the wall, smiling for a photo with the girls, when I notice a sharply dressed man from a distance. He sticks out like a sore thumb dressed in such a nice suit. He doesn't have to get much closer for my heart to feel like it drops out of my chest.

Luke.

He's heading this way. The closer he gets, the more I feel like I can't breathe. Why does he have to be so forget-how-to-breathe beautiful?

He's close enough for me to see his face clearer now. A small smile forms on his face.

If anyone is talking to me right now, I have no clue. The world around me ceases to exist as he approaches.

"Hi," he says when he reaches me.

"Hi."

"Congratulations, Princess," he whispers as he leans in and kisses my forehead.

"Thank you," I reply, barely able to form a single thought.

Luke looks behind me and nods his head. "Ladies. Congratulations."

"Thanks, Professor Luke," Tricia says, then realizes our parents are watching and he just kissed my forehead. "Uhhh...I mean, Luke. Thanks...Luke."

I look over at my dad who doesn't look too happy at the moment. Veronica is holding his hand as she whispers something in his ear and then offers me a wink.

I don't know what she just said, but his shoulders visibly relax. Although, he still doesn't look excited. I don't know what to do. I'm utterly thrilled that Luke is here, but by the look on my dad's face, he's going to ruin this day for me.

"Mr. Davis," Luke says as he turns to my father. "Can I have a word alone with you?"

What? No! Fuck, no!

Why does he want to talk to my dad...ALONE?

Nothing good can come from this.

"Oh, I don't think that's the best idea," I say as I step forward.

Luke looks between my father and me. "I would really love to have a word with you in private. If you would give me the opportunity."

My dad looks at me then at Luke and nods his head in agreement.

They walk away and if I thought I was sweating before, that was nothing compared to what's going on underneath my gown at the moment.

"It's gonna be okay," Veronica whispers to me.

"How do you know that?" I ask.

"Because I've had several conversations about this in the last week. He'll get there, just give him time. This is good...I'm impressed your man is so brave."

I roll my eyes. "A little warning would've been nice."

Shannon laughs. "I think this is awesome. I've never seen Mr. D so worked up before."

"Oh, my God, Shannon. Read the freakin' room," Aubrey whispers.

"What?" Shannon asks. "I'm just trying to lighten the mood. I don't think Luke and Mr. D are going to be brawling or anything."

I look over at them. Luke is talking while my dad has his hands in his pants pocket. I can't get a read on what's being said or how it's going. My dad nods his head a couple times. Is that a good thing?

It feels like they've been talking for hours instead of only a couple of minutes.

"Come on, let's just give them their space," Veronica suggests. "Let's get a photo with you ladies holding up your diplomas."

It's not the most subtle attempt to distract me, and it doesn't work. My eyes are glued to Luke and my dad. I'm guessing every photo I will be looking off in the distance with a fake smile.

At some point, the girls pull me in another direction so I can't see them. Somewhere in that time, Luke snuck up behind me.

I turn around and he's standing there.

"You're here," I say surprised.

He laughs. "Where else would I go?"

"I don't know. I started picturing calling the cops to get my dad off you."

"You've got quite the imagination."

"You know," I say as I rest a hand on my hip. "You could've warned me you were gonna do that."

He smiles. "Where's the fun in that?" I raise an eyebrow at him, not amused. "Ok. But I didn't know until last night. I hadn't had a plan yet, but I knew I needed your dad's permission if we were going to be together."

"Did...did you get it?" I breathe.

He lightly tugs on a piece of my hair. "You guys are going out to lunch but I'd love it if you come to my house after. We can talk then."

"Uh...okay."

"Perfect," he says. "First, let's get a quick photo of me and the graduate."

He pulls his phone out and holds it up. We both get in the frame and smile.

"I'll see you soon," he says then winks and walks away.

I'm left standing here, not sure what just happened.

He seems happy. He invited me over to his house. My dad is laughing with the other parents right now, not looking pissed off.

Did he just convince my dad in the matter of minutes to give him permission to be with me?

Chapter Thirty

Luke

I smile to myself as I walk away from her. She's definitely not sure what just happened, and as much as I want to talk to her now, she needs the time to finish her celebration with her friends and family.

I don't want to get in the way of that.

Looking down at the picture we just took, I realize I snapped two. One accidentally when she was looking up at me. Our eyes are trained on each other, you can see the admiration we both have for each other.

I click on the photo and make it my home screen.

When I was getting in bed last night, I got a notification in my email that graduation was today. It dawned on me, today was the perfect opportunity to get in front of her father.

Did he give me permission? Yes. Did I basically lay it all out there that I'm madly in love with his daughter and am going to marry her one day? Absolutely.

He's still a bit weary. I can sense it...but he doesn't know me yet. The more he gets to know me, gets to see me with his daughter, I think his trust will grow.

For now, that's enough for me.

When I get home and am greeted by a rowdy Vino, I realize I forgot to tell Savannah to bring Bailey. I grab my phone and text her to do so.

Now I need to take a shower. It was hot out, I was wearing a suit, and I was asking a man who doesn't like me to let me date his daughter. I was sweating my ass off.

It's around three when I get a text message from Savannah. I've basically cleaned my entire house, even though I pay cleaners to do that, that's how much energy I have coursing through me.

This has been five months in the making. The moment where I get to take her, claim her as mine, with no guilt or anything holding me back, it's *finally* here.

My doorbell rings and Vino trots alongside me. I have to refrain from running to open it. When I do, she's there in a white cotton dress.

She smiles at me, but before I can get a word in, Bailey and Vino jump at each other with excitement.

"Okay, guys," I say. "Let's take this outside."

I look at Savannah for her agreement. We walk through my house and go out the back door so the dogs can run around together.

Vino is over the moon. She missed her best friend.

Is it too soon to ask her to move in with me?

I know it is, but I just want a life together like this. Our dogs playing together while we enjoy our time together.

"Bailey missed her," she says as we take a seat on the covered couches outside.

"I think Vino has been clinically depressed since Bailey left."

Savannah's lips pout with a sad face.

It reminds me how much I want to taste her lips again. I look over at the dogs who are nowhere close to done playing.

"Come with me," I tell her as I extend my hand.

She takes it and I walk back into the house then down the hall to my bedroom. As soon as we cross the barrier into my room, I spin her around and bring her lips to mine.

She instantly moans into my mouth.

"We haven't even talked yet," she whispers through our kiss.

"After, baby," I say. "I need you first."

She wraps her arms around my neck and brings our mouths back together for a searing kiss. Any doubt I had about whether she would demand we speak first is gone as she pushes me further into the room.

My hands are all over her body, not sure where to touch first. I slide them from her ass up her hips, to the sides of her breasts then run back down until I can grip her ass.

"I think this is going to be quick," I growl as I bite her neck. "I need my dick inside of you. We can take our time later."

She pushes me down on the bed. I laugh as I fall onto my comforter. She makes quick work of her dress and underwear until she is completely naked.

"Take off your clothes," she instructs.

Shit, if this is how she's going to be, all dominant and brave, I'm not gonna last a minute. But fuck if I'm gonna stop her. Instead, I follow directions and get rid of my clothes.

I'm leaning back on my elbows as she starts to advance on me. She cups her breasts and massages them on her way.

My dick leaks precum at the sight. I think I could come without any stimulation to my dick by just watching her.

Her knees hit the mattress as she straddles me. One of her hands reaches for my cock and gives it a couple tugs. Then she starts to run it up and down her soaked pussy.

Fuck. I've never felt so completely owned by somebody else, both body and soul. It's terrifying and yet exactly where I want to be.

When she has my tip coated in her arousal, she starts to sink down onto me. I reach for her and grip one side of her hips. My thumb reaches for her clit and starts to rub circles around it.

She moans her appreciation as she descends all the way down until our bodies are completely joined together.

I love seeing her jaw fall as she tries to adjust to the feeling of me inside of her.

I move my other hand to her other hip as she starts to work her way up my dick then slams down fast. My hands grip her tight. There are no words that could explain what this feels like.

As she starts to work herself up and down, getting comfortable with her pace, I guide her with my hands.

"You look so damn beautiful taking me like this. I could watch my dick slide in and out of your pussy all day."

She moans at my words then starts to play with her breasts again.

The view in front of me is incredible, but I need to be closer to her when we come. I need to swallow her moans.

I wrap my hand around the back of her neck and lead her down until our lips meet.

She keeps up her pace, but this time I'm able to lift my hips and meet her with every thrust. We work in perfect sync with each other, I slam harder each time, awarding me with losing her breath a bit while we kiss.

I love knocking into her so hard that she gasps. It's my undoing.

"Fuck, I'm coming, baby," I whisper.

"I'm close," she answers.

Our lips join back together and don't let up as I pump my release into her warm pussy. I continue thrusting after I'm done then feel her pussy grip me as her own orgasm takes hold.

It seems to go on forever, long enough to make my dick slightly harden all over again. But I know we need some time to talk before we go for another round.

When she's done, the sexiest smile takes over her face.

"Hi, beautiful," I say.

"Hi."

"I missed you, Princess."

She leans down for a quick kiss. "I missed you, too."

"What do you say we get something to drink and join the dogs outside?"

"I think that sounds perfect," she replies.

We both clean up and get dressed, taking our time, stealing kisses along the way. Fuck, this feels so good, so right.

Who the hell would've thought a temporary teaching gig would have led me to the best thing that's ever happened to me?

I grab some iced tea and bring the drinks outside where she's already sitting on the couch petting the doggies.

They both have their tongues hanging out, looking happy as can be.

"Thank you," she says as I hand her a drink then join her.

"So…" I take a sip. "I guess we have some catching up to do."

"I think so."

"I'm trying to think of where to start."

"Let's start with what you said to my dad," she replies quickly.

I smile. "Has it been eating you up?"

"Well, he wouldn't let it out at lunch." She throws a hand up in the air. "He said you would probably want to talk first."

I nod my head in agreement. "True. I would like to be the one to talk about it first."

Her eyes open wide, like she's waiting for me to go on already.

"Okay," I start. "Well, last night I got this email from the school about graduation today. I knew I wanted to be with you, for real, in every way possible," I say, and her cheeks turn red. I reach up and run a finger down one of them, loving the combination of embarrassment and freshly fucked on her. "But I also knew you and your dad are close, and I would never want to be the one to change that. So, I decided weeks ago that if this was going to continue, I had to get his permission first. Graduation seemed like the perfect opportunity to get in front of him."

"It was risky," she admits.

"It was. He definitely could've yelled or refused to hear me out. But I was willing to risk the humiliation. I thought that if I just got in front of him, he could change his mind."

"What did you say?"

I take a deep breath. This part feels scarier than talking with her dad. This is the part where I lay my feelings out there entirely, not knowing if she feels the same way yet.

"I told him that I love you." She gasps, but I need to get it all out, so I continue. "I told him I've never met anyone like you. That from the moment I saw you, I knew you were different from everyone else I've ever met. That as I got to know you, I started to fall for everything about you. That what I love most about you is your heart. How you care so deeply for those around you, but how I want to be the one to show you that you deserve all the love in the world, because I don't think you believe it fully yet. I told him that one day, with his blessing of course, I was going to marry you."

There, I said it all. She has sunglasses so I can't see her eyes, but I see tears start to drip underneath her lenses and run down her cheeks. I need to know if these are happy tears.

I reach up and pull her glasses off her face. Her beautiful green eyes are glistening, but she smiles at me.

"You said all of that?"

"I did."

When her arms wrap around me and her head falls on my shoulder, my breaths start to come easier again. I wrap her up in my arms and enjoy her warmth.

"I love you, too," she cries.

"You do?"

She pulls away. "Of course. Did you doubt that?"

"I was a little worried you weren't there yet," I admit.

"I've been there for a while. Possibly since the moment I laid my eyes on you."

I kiss her lips. "I think it may be the same for me too."

"What did he say?" she asks.

I lean back on the couch and bring her down with me, wrapping my arms around her.

"He said he still has his reservations, but that he doesn't think it has to do with me. He said he thinks it's more his issue of letting go, trusting you and your decisions, and being okay with knowing you're an adult now. He gave me his permission though."

Her hands rest on my arm that's lying across her chest.

"Thank you for doing that. I'm sure it meant a lot to him. It means a lot to me."

"He's your father. I want nothing but the best for you, and having him approve of your boyfriend is pretty important."

We rest in silence for some time as we watch the dogs chase each other around the yard. They stop and drink water every so often before getting back at it.

"You know, when people ask how we met, what are we gonna say?" she asks.

I look down at her and smile. "We tell them the truth. I'll never regret or shy away from our story. It's where we met, where we fell in love, where our lives changed forever."

"I agree."

Epilogue

Luke

Two Years Later

"You ready for this?" I stop Savannah at the door of my parents' house.

She looks up at me with a smile, one that seems to be permanently stuck on her face since we found out. I lean down for a small kiss before we walk into the craziness.

"I'm so ready," she says. "It's been killing me to keep in the news."

"Then after you, Mrs. Giannelli," I say as I playfully swat her ass.

She may be pregnant, but she's still my sexy wife, who I can't seem to keep my hands off of. She doesn't even flinch at the contact of my hand on her behind. I think that's how you know she's used to it. We've been married for a year, but you'd think it was a day. I still feel like the luckiest guy in the world.

I proposed to her on one of our work trips to Italy, bringing her back to Mancini Farms, where it all began. She's been working for us for a year now. She came in for a formal interview with my siblings, and they were sold instantly. She was hesitant at first, not wanting to be hired because of our relationship.

It took some convincing, but she eventually agreed. She's been a huge asset to our company. Her people skills are second to none, and she loves the travel. I love seeing her happy, so it all works out.

Her father and I have a solid relationship now. It took about six months before things started to feel a bit more natural.

"Hello?" I shout as we walk into the house, but nobody hears me.

The voices coming from the family room are too loud to beat. To a stranger, it probably sounds like my family is yelling at each other, but this is how Italians talk. I know it's just a regular Sunday conversation.

We walk into the room, and I spot my two-year-old nephew, Joey, playing on the ground with his toys. He sees me, and a huge smile breaks out. Joey and Sienna are my brother Gabe's kids.

"Hey, buddy," I say as I pick him up and kiss his cheek.

His chubby arm wraps around my neck while he points to his trucks on the floor.

"I play trucks," he says.

"Wow. Look at all those trucks lined up," I say as I put him back down.

Savannah is already sitting with Mia and Alexis as they chat and laugh together. It's been great to see the three of them form such a tight bond. I couldn't have asked for a better person to bring into my family.

Sienna and Ma are in the kitchen laughing at something, and I turn around to see flour on Sienna's face. The girl is growing up too fast. She's already eight, but sometimes I swear she acts like an adult. Ma loves having Sienna in the kitchen because she's talented and enjoys it as much as she does.

Looking back at Savannah, her eyes are locked on me with worry. Oh, shit, she isn't feeling good. We were worried she'd be running to the bathroom to puke before we got the news out. I don't know why they call it morning sickness. My girl is getting sick around the clock, and there's not a damn thing I can do to stop it. I've researched all the ways to help ease the vomiting, but nothing works. I'm left powerless, seeing her suffer through this. I hate it.

It's a good indication that I'm gonna have a hard time watching her in pain while she gives birth.

I know she's trying to tell me we need to get the news out now so she can openly get sick all evening.

"Hey, Ma," I turn toward the kitchen and shout. She looks up at me. "Can you and Sienna come over here for a second? Real quick?"

Her eyes look concerned, but she puts down her spoon.

When she and Sienna come in, she sits on the couch's armrest where Pa is lounging next to Marcus. I thought Savannah would join me, but she's looking worse by the second, so I guess I just need to come out with it.

"Everybody," I start. "Savannah and I have some news to share. There will be another baby to spoil by Christmas. We're pregnant!"

Just as expected, the women are jumping up and down screaming while the men in the family shake my hand. I am lost in the sea of people, trying to find Savannah, who is crowded around the women, and she pushes past everybody and runs to the bathroom.

"Gonna be sick, sorry," she screams along the way.

The women in the room are wearing sympathetic looks, while the men are a little more disgusted. I hate to think that she's alone getting sick.

"I'll be right back. You guys start dinner without us. I'm not sure how much she'll be able to get down anyway," I say, then head for the bathroom.

When I get there, I lightly tap on the door.

"Babe?" she questions.

"It's me."

"Come in."

I open the door to see her on her knees with her head resting on her arm, which is draped over the toilet.

"Did you get sick?"

She nods her head up and down. I grab a hand towel from the shelf, wet it with some cool water, and then join her on the floor. Her eyes look heavy as I start to dab the towel on her forward and around her cheeks.

"I'm sorry, baby. I wish there was something more I can do."

"It's fine," she whispers. "The doctor said it typically clears up around twelve weeks. Hopefully, it's over by next week."

"You look exhausted, babe. Let's just go home so you can get rest."

She shakes her head. "No, I'll just rest on the couch. We just told your family. I don't want to leave without giving you guys a chance to celebrate."

That's Savannah for you. She's the most selfless person I've ever met. She has gotten better and has found her worth and her voice. But she doesn't think of herself enough.

"I'm serious," she says.

She can also read me like a book, knowing exactly what's going through my mind.

"Fine," I agree. "We can stay. But I want you to let me know the second you feel like going home."

"Ok. I love you."

I smile. "I love you," I tell her, then look down at her belly. "I love both of you."

I try not to get emotional, but it's hard when your wife is carrying your baby. I still look at her and just feel completely in awe.

I help her clean up, and we walk back to the family room. Everybody is gathered around the table, so I bring her to the couch and make sure she's comfortable.

"Go. Please have dinner and enjoy the night with your family," she tells me as she snuggles up in a blanket.

I hesitantly agree and sit next to Marcus and across from Gabe. All eyes are on me as I sit down.

"How is she?" Ma asks. "I feel just awful that she isn't feeling well."

"She's alright. Probably won't be eating anything tonight. She just wants to rest."

"Has she been getting sick a lot?" Alexis asks.

"Every day for weeks now. I just want it to be over so she can enjoy this pregnancy."

"How far along is she?" Gabe asks.

"Eleven weeks."

"Well, it should be over soon," Ma offers.

"That's what the doctor said," I tell her. "I'm hoping."

"Well, I say we offer up a toast," Pa says as he holds up his wine. "To our newest addition to the family. We'll be waiting anxiously to meet you."

"Hear, hear!" Marcus shouts. "To Savannah and Luke."

We clink our glasses together. It feels good to finally get the news out to the family. Savannah has been struggling at work to keep on an act, pretending to feel fine when she's been anything but.

"This makes sense now," Mia says. "I thought she has had the stomach bug or something with all the time she's been spending in the bathroom at work."

I wince. "Yeah, work's been rough for her."

"You need to tell her she is to stay home for the next week and get some rest," Gabe interjects authoritatively. "I don't want her pushing herself too hard."

"I tried. Maybe now she'll listen since the news is out."

"Don't worry. I'll take care of it," he says like it's a done deal.

Gabe does know how to get what he wants. If he tells Savannah she needs to rest, she's going to rest.

After we finish dinner, we help Ma load the dishwasher and then file into the family room where Savannah is resting. She seems a little better now, though she still looks tired.

Alexis and Ma join her on the couch while Pa and Marcus play with Joey and Sienna on the floor.

"Did Mia tell you what Mr. Hansley said?" Gabe whispers over his shoulder.

I tense up at the mention of his name. "Fucking Marcus needs to learn to keep it in his pants. I can't believe he slept with Mr. Hansley's friend's daughter."

Mr. Hansley is a large client of ours out of Chicago, who is pretty furious with what he thinks our brand represents. Apparently, Marcus slept with his friend's daughter and then ghosted her. I don't know the whole story, but I do know he's hosting a big charity event, one of our wines will be the star of the menu that night...if Marcus doesn't fuck it up somehow in the meantime.

"He said he wants to see Marcus prove to him that he's a man worth doing business with," Gabe mutters. "I don't know what the hell to do about that. This guy is acting old school, like our personal lives reflect how we do business."

"Marcus isn't gonna like this," I tell him.

"Well, tough shit. The guy needs to learn to keep it in his pants for once. Now it's affecting our business."

"I have an idea," Mia whispers, making me jump enough to almost spill the contents of my coffee all over myself.

"Geez, Mia. You're such a creeper," I mutter under my breath.

"Oh, please, you two gossips over here are less than subtle."

Gabe rolls his eyes at her. "What's your idea?"

"We tell him the truth like grown-ass adults and stop whispering in the corner about it like little children."

"We're just trying to protect him," I defend.

"Well, he's his own person. He doesn't need protecting. We just need to tell him what's going on this week. He can take it, and he might even figure out how to clear it all up on his own."

"Fine. Whatever, we'll talk about it later. Right now, I just want to check on my wife," I bite out.

I walk over to her, where Sienna is now snuggling on her belly, telling the baby she can't wait to meet it. Also, it's super awkward to not know the sex of the baby. I keep calling it...it.

Finally, after some small talk and questions about the due date, Savannah looks over at me and gives me the *it's time to leave* look.

"Alright, everybody. I know it's a bit early for us, but we need to head out so Savannah can get some more rest."

I hold out my hand for her. She takes it, and I pull her up and into my arm so I can hold onto her.

We head toward the door while everybody continues to shout their *congratulations* and *feel betters* as we walk away. I keep my grip on Savannah the entire way to the car. She leans her head on my arm as we walk. When we get to the car, I kiss her forehead before helping her in.

Her eyes are closed before I get settled in.

I smile as I turn the key and slowly pull out of the driveway. Every minute or so, I look over at her, and my heart feels like it skips a beat.

I often think back to the moment she walked into my classroom. The instant electricity that coursed through me at the mere sight of her. It was as if my body knew immediately that she would be my wife. I'm just damn proud that we made it through the semester first before we started a relationship, even though everything in me wanted her no matter what the consequences. Well, there was our time in Italy, but as Savannah still reminds me to this day, "It doesn't count...it was Italy. Even Monica and Chandler agree."

Marcus and Lexi

Are you ready for Marcus and Lexi's story next?

Where We Fall is coming to you on December 8th, 2023.

A sexy *fake relationship* romance that you won't want to miss.

Click on the link below to pre-order your copy today!

Pre-Order here!

Signed Paperback

Do you want a signed copy for your book collection?

NICOLE BAKER

Click on the link below to purchase a signed copy of any of my books to add to your library!!

www.nicolebakerauthor.com

Follow the Author

To have access to a Bonus Scene with Luke and Savannah– visit my website and subscribe to my newsletter with *Bonus Scene* written in the message!

www.nicolebakerauthor.com

Facebook @nicolebakerauthor

Instagram @nicolebaker_author

TikTok @authornicolebaker

Also By Nicole Baker

Made in United States
Cleveland, OH
11 December 2024

11688412R10173